ROWAN
and the ZEBAK

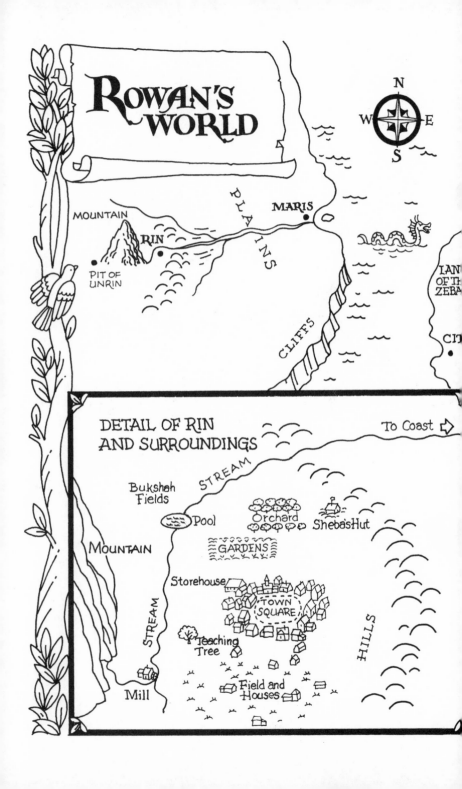

EMILY RODDA

ROWAN
and the ZEBAK

Greenwillow Books

An Imprint of HarperCollins*Publishers*

Library of Congress Cataloging-in-Publication Data

Rodda, Emily.
Rowan and the Zebak / Emily Rodda.
p.   cm.
"Greenwillow Books."
Sequel to: Rowan and the Keeper of the Crystal.
Summary: After a flying lizard carries off his little sister, Rowan of Rin
and three companions are guided by a rhyming riddle on a journey to the
land of their old enemy, the Zebak, in order to rescue her.
ISBN 0-06-029778-6(trade).   ISBN 0-06-029779-4 (lib. bdg.)
[1. Heroes—Fiction.   2. Riddles—Fiction.   3. Fantasy.]   I. Title.
PZ7.R5996 Rn 2002   [Fic]—dc21   00-052796

1   2   3   4   5   6   7   8   9   10   First American Edition

For Penny Matthews,
valued editor,
with thanks

AUTHOR'S NOTE

Thanks to all the Rowan fans who wrote to me
suggesting a book called *Rowan and the Zebak*.
I hope you enjoy reading this story as much
as I enjoyed writing it.

CONTENTS

1 ∿ THE WARNING

The grach flew west, following the scent. It had flown for a long time and it was tired and hungry, but it did not think of feeding or stopping to rest. There was no thought at all behind its flat yellow eyes. Just one fixed idea. To follow the scent, reach the place it had been told to reach, and take back to its masters what it had been told to take.

The grach was called Bara, and it was a hundred and twenty years old. It had been trained well. Not kindly, perhaps, but cleverly, and for many, many years. The idea never entered its mind that now, far away from the whips and shouts of its masters, it could choose what it did.

The sea had been left behind long ago, and dimly the grach was aware that below it now were rolling green hills and a winding stream glinting bright in the sunlight. It was aware that a mountain, its peak hidden in cloud, rose in the blue distance ahead.

But its eyes were not important now. Its ears, closed against the rushing of the wind and the beating of its own wings, were not important, either. All that was important was its forked tongue, flickering in and out, tasting the air, tasting the scent.

It knew it was close to its goal. The scent was stronger—the warm animal scent that made its jaws drip with hunger. Bukshah. It even knew the name.

"Bukshah," its masters had said, so many times, flourishing the gray woolly hide in front of its face, feeding it bloody pieces of meat so that the delicious taste mingled with the hide smell. When they had sent it away on this quest they had said it again. "Bukshah. Seek." And then they had loosed its chain.

The bukshah scent was strong, but there were other scents, too. Some the grach had tasted before, one it had not. The one it had not tasted was full of danger. It was fire, snow, and ice. It was hot breath, dripping fangs, and ancient, jealous power.

The leathery spines on the grach's back prickled with warning. But its yellow lizard eyes did not flicker, and the beating of its scaly mottled wings did not falter as it flew on, to Rin.

* * *

Rowan scanned the blue, blue sky above the village. It was still clear, except for the cloud that always shrouded the tip of the forbidden Mountain. And yet—surely a summer storm was brewing. How else could he explain his strange, nagging feeling that something unexpected and fearful was about to happen? The sense of dread had begun at midmorning, and had grown stronger every moment since.

It is nothing, he told himself firmly. He fought away the fear and did not speak of it to Jiller, his mother. Why worry her needlessly, today of all days?

Today Jiller should be as lighthearted as his little sister, Annad, who was already dancing around the cottage garden, thinking herself very fine in a new pink dress. She should be as plainly joyful as Strong Jonn, even now coming through the gate, swinging Annad into his arms and striding toward the house, splendid in his wedding finery.

Rowan made himself wave to Jonn, shout a greeting. And when the dark, fearful feeling stabbed at him yet again, he forced it down.

The hardworking people of Rin did not often lay aside their everyday cares for festivals and holidays. But even in Rin a wedding was a cause for celebration, and *this* wedding—the marriage of Strong

Jonn of the Orchard to Jiller of the Field—was a greater occasion than most.

Jonn and Jiller were well loved, and Jiller's son, Rowan of the Bukshah, was Rin's greatest hero, if its most unlikely one. Shy, dreamy, and timid though he was, he had conquered the forbidden Mountain and faced the Dragon that reigned at its peak. He had allied himself with the wandering Travelers to save Rin from a terrible fate. And it was whispered that he was joined to the fishlike Maris people on the coast by his strange bond with their mysterious leader, the Keeper of the Crystal.

Once the most disappointing child in the village, Rowan was now respected. No one teased or criticized him these days. No one told him he was too old to be the keeper of the gentle bukshah.

He was even feared by some, who thought he had unnatural powers. Such people stopped speaking when Rowan came into the storehouse or passed by a meeting place, and they warned their children not to annoy him. When a black bukshah calf was born in spring—black, instead of the usual soft gray—such people whispered that it was an omen, a sign of Rowan's power.

If anyone had told them that Rowan wanted nothing more than to be accepted as one of them, that this was all he had ever wanted, they would have laughed.

It was largely because of Rowan that this marriage was more than a simple village celebration. Yesterday the three great Traveler kites, their riders dangling beneath them, had appeared in the sky above the valley. Since then, the tribe that always followed them had made camp on the hills, ready to join the party and make music. Perlain of Pandellis had come from Maris to represent his people and bring gifts. He had left the sea and the salt spray of his home gladly, though Maris skin dried and cracked quickly inland, and the journey had not been comfortable for him.

This day was important enough to tempt the stolid millers, Val and Ellis, from their mill. It had even caused gruff, solitary Bronden the furniture maker to shut her work shed for the day. No one wanted to miss the celebration or fail to pay their respects.

So at noon, when Jiller and Jonn walked with Rowan and Annad to the great tree above the bukshah field, a crowd was waiting. Only Sheba, the village wise woman, had kept away and stayed crouching alone in her hut beyond the orchard. No one was surprised at that, and everyone was secretly glad. For Sheba, though sought out by many in times of sickness or danger, would have been an uncomfortable wedding guest.

As he entered the tree's welcome shade, Rowan was only half aware of Annad dancing excitedly beside him, of Jonn and Jiller walking ahead, and of the crowd staring. The feeling of dread was growing stronger, clouding his mind, darkening his thoughts, making him silent and watchful.

He gritted his teeth, trying to make sure the darkness did not show. Everyone in Rin is happy, ready to celebrate, he told himself. Why should I be different?

You have always been different, a voice at the back of his mind said. And now more than ever.

Angrily he pushed the voice away. He turned his head and caught sight of Ogden the storyteller, the leader of the Travelers, standing with his adopted daughter, Zeel, and the rest of the tribe at one side of the crowd.

Beside the people of Rin, sober even when dressed in their best, the Travelers looked as bright as birds in their vivid silks, their long, curling hair threaded with ribbons, beads, and feathers. But with a stab of fear Rowan saw that their faces were watchful. They were standing very still, as though every muscle in their lean brown bodies was poised for flight. And Ogden's deep-set eyes were grave.

Jonn and Jiller noticed nothing. They smiled and bowed to the Travelers, and Ogden bowed low in return. But his dark gaze looked beyond them to Rowan, and in his eyes was a question. Rowan knew what it was.

Something is wrong in the land. We feel it. You feel it, too. I can see you do. What is it?

Rowan shook his head slightly. *I do not know.*

Ogden's eyes flicked to the front of the crowd where Perlain, the Maris man, stood with Allun the baker and Marlie the weaver, Jonn and Jiller's great friends.

Marlie and Allun were smiling, handing flowers to Jiller. But Perlain, small and glistening in his closely fitting blue garments, stood stiffly, his webbed hands pressed tightly to his sides. The hood that helped to protect him from the drying sun had been pushed back as a sign of respect, so Rowan could see that his flat, glassy eyes were fixed and staring.

Perlain was afraid. But what was there to be afraid of, here under this green shade, in this protected valley?

There is danger, Rowan. Danger in the land.

The message suddenly rang clearly in Rowan's mind. It was the Keeper of the Crystal in Maris, warning him, as he had warned Perlain.

But already Jonn and Jiller were standing before old Lann, and the ceremony had begun.

I cannot say anything now, Rowan thought desperately. If I even try, no one will listen, however much they say I am a hero. They will think I am trying to stop the marriage. Mother and Jonn will think so, too. I cannot do it.

There was a time when he had hated the thought that Jonn might take the place of Sefton, his father. But now he knew that no one would ever take Sefton's place—in Jiller's heart, or his. It was just that hearts were big enough to accept more loves than one. And Strong Jonn of the Orchard, his father's friend, was his friend, too.

He had never said this to Jiller or to Jonn. In Rin it was thought a sign of weakness to discuss feelings openly. Only by appearing happy at this wedding could Rowan show how glad he was that it was taking place.

There was someone else to consider, as well. Rowan glanced at his little sister standing wide-eyed beside him. Annad had never known their father, who had died when she was just a baby. She adored Jonn. She had looked forward so much to this day. She had loved the idea of dressing up and parading in front of the village.

I cannot do it, he thought again. I cannot break

this moment. Perlain and Ogden are content to wait. So I will be content also. What harm can there be in waiting just a little?

Bitterly, bitterly, in the days that followed did Rowan wish he had decided differently.

2 ∽ THE ATTACK

There was silence under the great tree as Jonn and Jiller made their final vows. Then, as Lann pronounced them husband and wife, there was a loud burst of clapping, cheering, and congratulations.

The Rin adults clustered around and took Jonn and Jiller off to the feast that had been set up nearby, courteously making sure that Perlain and the Travelers were swept along with the tide. Annad leaped to join her friends as though a spring had been released inside her. Rowan stayed where he was, watching.

Jonn and Jiller sat down at the head of the main feasting table, laughing and talking. All the tables were loaded with the best the village could provide. Platters were piled high with fruits and salad vegetables, the best bukshah cheese, the softest bread rolls that Allun and his mother, Sara, could fashion, and toffees, jellies, and cakes of every kind from Solla the sweets maker. Great cool jugs of hoopberry juice and slip-daisy wine stood here and there.

The Travelers' music began. Ogden must have decided that it was best to continue with the festivities as though nothing were wrong. Rowan leaned against the smooth trunk of the great tree, trying to order his thoughts. Sunlight sparkled through the leaves, flecking the ground with spots of gold.

Under this green canopy the people of Rin had married, named their children, and farewelled their dead since they had first arrived in the valley three hundred years ago. The tree had been large then. Now it was a giant.

"Rowan! Look!" Annad's piercing voice rose above the music, the talk of the adults, and the giggling of her friends.

Rowan glanced around. Annad was standing by the fence, looking down at the bukshah field. She beckoned to him excitedly. "Come and see!" she called.

He walked down to join her. Her friends grew silent and moved back shyly as he approached, but Annad ran to him, seized his arm, and pulled him toward the fence.

"They are dancing!" she laughed, pointing.

Rowan caught his breath in surprise. The humped gray beasts had arranged themselves, side by side, shoulder to shoulder, into a tight circle. Their heavy heads all faced outward. Their bodies were pressed together so closely that their manes seemed joined. Many were pawing the ground. At first glance it really did look as though they were doing some sort of dance.

Annad was jumping up and down. "Rowan, come on!" she squealed, tugging at his hand. "Come down and see them with me!"

"No, Annad." Rowan smiled. Much as he would have liked to leave the gathering for the bukshah field, he knew that it would seem odd and impolite if he did.

Annad exclaimed impatiently and pulled her hand away from his. She shook off her soft shoes and, heedless of her fine clothes, clambered through the fence and began running across the field beyond.

"Annad!" called Rowan. But the little girl took no notice. He smiled and shook his head as he watched her jump the stream and run toward the bukshah, calling to Star, their leader. Her hair flew like spun gold around her head. Her pink dress billowed in the faint breeze. She looked like a huge butterfly fluttering across the grass.

Rowan expected the bukshah to break out of their strange formation when Annad disturbed them, but to his surprise there was no movement from the herd at all. They stood like rocks, their noses up, sniffing the air.

Rowan stared in puzzlement. And then something else struck him. Where were the young bukshah—the calves that had been born in the spring? He could not see them anywhere. Even the black one, the smallest of all, was missing.

Annad was dancing toward Star now, chattering to her, stretching out her hand. Rowan jumped with shock as Star rumbled warningly and roughly jerked her head, pushing Annad away.

Star was always so gentle. The smallest child in Rin could lead her. She loved Annad almost as much as she loved Rowan himself. Yet she seemed to be trying to keep Annad away from the herd.

Rowan frowned, gripping the fence. Or—was Star trying to make Annad run back to where she had come from? To shelter. To safety—

"Annad!" he called urgently. But his voice was drowned by the music and laughter around the feasting tables, and Annad did not hear.

He saw her hesitate for a moment, then take a step forward and again stretch out her hand. This time the jerk of Star's head was hard enough to send her tumbling onto the grass. The huge beasts on Star's left and right pawed the ground but did not leave their places.

They will not break the circle, thought Rowan. And suddenly he understood why. The calves were inside, enclosed and hidden by a wall of strong adult bodies.

A terrible fear gripped him. He scrambled awkwardly through the fence and started to run toward the stream. "Annad!" he shouted. "Annad! Beware!"

But already it was too late. What happened next took only moments, but afterward to the end of his life, Rowan would always remember it as though it had taken long, long minutes.

He was running, running, his chest aching with breathless fear, but he could not run fast enough. He saw Annad turning toward him as she clambered to her feet, brushing at her dress. He saw her pink, annoyed face, her spun gold hair, suddenly darkened by a rushing shadow that blocked the sun.

He heard a terrible wakening roar from the peak of the Mountain, and an answering defiant, rasping hiss from the sky above. He heard the rush of wings and the bellowing of the bukshah as a huge shape plummeted toward them—a creature mottled green, yellow, and gray, spiked and hideous, with three lashing tails. He heard his own cry of warning, and Annad's high-pitched scream as she realized her danger and began to run, her dress whipping and tangling in the wind created by the mighty wings.

Rowan leaped the stream, shouting in terror, shouting to Annad to drop to the ground, hide herself in the long grass. But he knew, even as he called, that Annad was hearing and understanding nothing but her own need to escape.

With horror he saw the beast's flat yellow eyes slide to one side and fix themselves on the small, fluttering, running figure, bright pink and gold against the green field. For an instant the creature hovered, and around its neck Rowan caught a glimpse of something that astonished and bewildered him.

Then his mind was wiped clear by panic. The creature was turning in the air, wheeling away from the bukshah and plunging instead toward Annad, its huge red talons reaching for her.

"No!" Rowan hurled himself forward, waving his arms, shrieking at the beast, trying to distract it, to make it turn again. But in an instant it had swooped, and then, its great wings beating with a noise like thunder, it was hissing in triumph, speeding away.

Its burden was light and slowed it not at all. In seconds it was a dark spot above the distant hills. In minutes it had disappeared from sight.

And Annad had gone with it.

3 ∽ THE DECISION

"We must go after the beast. Attack it where it lands."

"We cannot leave the village unde-fended. It may come again."

"But Annad—"

"The child is gone. Gone. There is nothing to be done."

Huddled on the ground, numb with misery, Rowan heard the voices around him. Familiar voices. Sara. Old Lann. Marlie. Bronden.

He clambered to his feet and stared around, dazed. People had come running from the feast tables. Now they clustered together, shocked and bewildered, their festival clothes rumpled, their good shoes sinking into the long, rich grass of the field. There was no sign of the Travelers or of Perlain.

Jiller, all the color drained from her face, was standing very straight. Jonn was close beside her, but she did not lean on him. That was not her way.

Old Lann turned to her. "What do you want of us, Jiller of the Field?" she asked formally.

"Nothing." Jiller spoke through lips that barely moved. "There is nothing to be done. Annad is gone."

"No!" The word burst from Rowan before he could stop it.

His mother turned to him. Her eyes were black with grief.

"She is gone, Rowan," she repeated. "You saw the creature take her. By now she is dead."

Rowan shook his head. "We—we do not know that," he stammered. "The beast . . . was not wild, but tame."

There was a moment's shocked silence, then Lann hobbled up to him. "What do you mean?" she demanded.

"It—it was wearing a collar. I saw. A metal collar, with a fastening for a chain," Rowan said.

Lann stared at him. Her face was creased into a thousand lines that showed her pain. She, too, had loved little Annad.

Rowan took a deep breath. "I believe—it came from over the sea," he said. He felt the eyes of all the villagers upon him, and his mother's eyes most of all. His face burned, but he made himself go on. "On the coast, the Keeper of the Crystal felt danger come. The Travelers, too, felt a strangeness in the land."

There was a whispering in the crowd.

"And you, Rowan?" Jiller's voice sounded flat and dead.

Rowan swallowed. This was the question he had been dreading. He bent his head and forced himself to speak. "I felt . . . something. A warning. But I thought . . . there was time . . ." His voice trailed away miserably. He looked up.

His mother's face had gone blank. "You said nothing to me of this," she said.

"I . . . felt I could not. I did not wish to spoil this day," Rowan mumbled.

Slowly Jiller nodded. Then she turned and walked away.

Marlie hurried after her, but Jonn lingered to put his hand on Rowan's shoulder. His face was furrowed with grief, but his voice was steady. "You could not have known, Rowan," he said. "Do not blame yourself. Come home with us now."

Rowan shook his head. He could not go home. He knew he would be no comfort to his mother. In her heart she must hate him for what he had done. For what he had *not* done.

Jonn hesitated. Then he squeezed Rowan's shoulder, and left him.

The crowd moved restlessly. Rowan caught sight of Allun standing to one side, his usually good-humored face tight and pale.

"If one creature has come here from across the sea, who is to say when more may follow?" someone called. "We must arm ourselves and prepare."

Timon the teacher took Jonn's place at Rowan's side. "Is there anything more that you can tell us, Rowan?" he asked urgently.

"We need to know nothing more," snapped Val the miller, towering shoulder to shoulder with her brother in the center of the crowd. "Who would tame such a beast to do their will? Who would collar it with metal rather than cloth or leather? Who would send it across the sea to attack us? It is the Zebak."

The hated name fell into the crowd like a stone into a still pond. A low muttering began, rippling outward.

"The Zebak were defeated in Maris, not long ago," Bree of the garden protested. "They suffered heavy losses. Would they try again so soon?"

"It could be that their leaders have at last decided that invasion by sea is too dangerous," Timon said.

"So they are testing a new way of attacking us—from the air."

The muttering rose to an angry babble, and many fists were clenched. Only the oldest of the people now living in Rin had battled the Zebak hand to hand. But all had seen pictures of cruel Zebak faces, brows marked with a black line running from hairline to nose. All knew that their ancestors had first come to this land as Zebak warrior slaves. All were ready to fight to keep their freedom.

As the noise around him increased, Rowan looked over to where Allun was standing. But Allun had gone.

Old Lann banged her stick on a rock and silence fell. "We will talk more of this," she said firmly. "But first we must clear the feasting tables, and take what food remains to the cool house. Nothing must be wasted. There may be hard times ahead."

Rowan stood silently as the crowd melted away to do her bidding.

"No doubt you did what you thought best, Rowan of the Bukshah," snorted Bronden as she passed him. "You and your Maris and Traveler friends—who, I notice, have fled at the first sign of danger. But perhaps another time you will think better of keeping special knowledge to yourself."

She was gone before he could answer.

"Your people do not understand how it is with you," a quiet voice said in his ear.

Rowan swung around to see Perlain standing beside him. The Maris man was dripping wet. "I did not want to intrude on your meeting," he explained. "And I was dry. So I soaked in the stream and listened. The man with clever eyes—he spoke wisely, I think."

"Timon. Yes," Rowan murmured.

"This episode may have been only a test," Perlain said calmly. "But, if so, the test has been successful. Soon the Zebak will have proof that their beast has been to Rin and back."

Rowan's mouth felt as dry as dust. He licked his lips. "Do you think it will deliver Annad to the Zebak—alive?" he asked finally. His heart had begun thudding like the pounding of a Traveler drum.

"Yes," said Perlain simply. "The Zebak have always preferred to take their captives alive."

Rowan shuddered in the warm sun as though chilled to the bone. His mind was a whirlwind of shock and grief, but at the center of the whirlwind was one clear thought. Annad was a captive because of him. Because he had not sounded a warning when first he sensed danger. Because he had let her go to the bukshah field alone. Because he had been too slow to reach her side before she was snatched away.

Perlain was regarding him thoughtfully. "You are very grieved," he said. "What can I give to help you?"

And suddenly Rowan knew.

"You can give me a boat, Perlain," he said. "I am returning to Maris with you. Then I am going to the place of the Zebak, to find my sister and bring her home."

Perlain shook his head. "You cannot do it, my friend. Such a journey would be filled with peril. And at its end you would only join your sister in her fate, without hope of escape."

He heard a sound behind him and jumped as he saw Star standing there. "Your bukshah wants your attention," he said nervously, moving aside.

Rowan rubbed Star's soft nose, taking comfort in her massive, woolly strength. She pushed against him and rumbled deep in her throat.

"Do not mourn," he whispered to her. "You did your best to warn Annad away from the field. And you protected the calves bravely. They were safe inside your circle."

"Does the creature understand your words?" asked Perlain curiously.

"She understands what I mean by them," said Rowan. He saw Star's nose twitch and whirled around to search the sky. But no dark shape loomed there—only a bright splash of yellow against the blue. It swooped lower and lower until the figure of the girl who swung from the great kite was clear. Zeel.

Star huffed gently in Rowan's ear. Turning, he saw Ogden the storyteller approaching across the field.

"The creature was far distant before we could reach our camp and launch the kite," Ogden called. "I fear Zeel lost sight of it. Her signal was of disappointment."

Rowan had heard no signal. But he would not have expected to. The Travelers' reed pipes made sounds that were too high for others to hear.

Zeel's feet touched the ground lightly. The kite billowed behind her, then fell into soft, bright folds. She gathered it up and strode toward them. Her hair had blown back from her face. Her straight brows were drawn together and her pale eyes were angry.

Rowan felt Perlain stiffen beside him. "Rowan! She is not a Traveler!" the Maris man hissed in his ear. "She does not have the black line tattoo on her brow—but still, she is Zebak! I see it now." His hand moved, feeling for the knife at his belt.

"Peace, Perlain," Rowan hastily whispered back. "Zeel is Zebak born, but she was washed up by the sea as a tiny child, and Ogden took her in. She can be trusted. She is as much a Traveler as any of her people. Believe me."

Perlain lowered his hand, but he remained watchful as Zeel joined them.

"I am sorry, Rowan of the Bukshah," she said. "The beast far outpaced me." She turned to Ogden. "It was as you thought. It turned and took the most direct way to the coast. It will be over the cliffs by now."

Rowan wet his dry lips.

"Will you go after it?" Zeel asked him almost casually, throwing the kite silk over her shoulder.

He nodded.

"This is foolishness," Perlain said coldly. "However brave a fish may be, it is doomed if it ventures into a serpent's lair."

"It will not be just one fish," snapped Zeel. "Rowan will have many companions. The people of Rin are—"

"No," Rowan interrupted hurriedly, feeling his face begin to burn. "I will be going alone."

Zeel looked startled and unbelieving.

"Perlain will arrange a boat for me." Rowan rushed on, in case Zeel, too, should begin to argue with him. "And if the Travelers could spare two kites and their riders to speed us to Maris, we will save much time."

He saw Perlain open his mouth in alarmed protest, but Ogden was already nodding agreement. "Tor may go to Maris," he said. "Tor and—"

"And me," Zeel broke in.

Ogden smiled slightly. "So—it is settled."

"It is madness!" said Perlain. "The seas between here and the land of the Zebak are treacherous. And even if by a miracle Rowan survives to reach the shore, what will he do then? Where will he go? No one can know."

Rowan thought about that, and his stomach seemed to turn over. "There is someone who might know," he said reluctantly.

How foolish, he thought, meeting Ogden's amused eyes, to be afraid of *this*, when the journey ahead is so perilous.

"Not so foolish," said Ogden, smiling, and Rowan realized with a shock that the storyteller had read his thoughts. "But you are wise to face your fear. The time the meeting may take will be well spent." He thought for a moment, stroking his chin, then looked up. "I must leave you," he said. "Zeel will accompany you to our camp when you are ready."

He bowed and left them.

Star nuzzled Rowan's neck, and he stroked her gently. "I am going far away, Star," he said in a low voice. "If I do not return, the people will appoint another keeper of the bukshah. Someone kind—do not fear. And in the meantime Mother will see to you—for my sake, and for Annad's."

Star's small, wise eyes regarded him gravely, as though she understood and was unhappy.

Rowan gave her a final pat, then turned quickly and walked with Zeel and the silent Perlain up to the orchard. They threaded their way through the whispering trees toward the small hut beyond. Rowan did not know what awaited him there. He only knew that if he was to find Annad, he needed help. And his only hope of help lay with Sheba.

The strange pale grass that grew outside the hut was unmarked except for a single set of footprints that led to the door.

"Your wise woman already has a visitor," Zeel said. "A man, I think, who treads fast and lightly, like a Traveler, but with heavier shoes, like those of Rin."

Rowan thought that Sheba's visitor might be the only person in Rin, apart from Sheba herself, who would let him go his own way without hindrance. Leaving Zeel and Perlain, he tiptoed across the grass, crept to the door of the hut and pressed his ear against it. A loud cackle of laughter rang out inside and he leaped back, shivering with fright, feeling six years old again.

"Come in, skinny rabbit," growled Sheba. "I have been waiting for you."

4 ⌒ THE GIFT

 Rowan entered the hut, straining his eyes to see in the gloom, choking a little at the thick smell of smoke, ash, dust, and bitter herbs that filled the room.

Sheba sat with her back to the door. She was holding her hands out to the fire, rubbing them as if to wash them in the dull red glow. On the other side of the fireplace stood her visitor. As Rowan had hoped, it was Allun. His face was pale with anger.

"The entertainment here has been poor," Sheba rasped without turning around. "This half-Traveler clown has not amused me with his whining tale. A brat lost through her own foolishness and her brother's weakness—pah! And now he has grown silent, sulking like a child himself. You will provide better sport, skinny rabbit."

She chuckled to herself and spread her bony fingers, admiring the long yellow nails that curved at the tips like claws.

Rowan struggled to keep calm, though her words hurt and angered him. He knew that it was part of Sheba's game to find her visitors' weakest points and prod at them. She liked to watch them first writhe, then give way to fear or fury.

"It seems that your tricks do not work with everyone, old woman," jeered Allun. "The boy is too strong for you."

Oh, Allun, be still, Rowan thought desperately. You do not understand how spiteful she is. But he did not dare to say a word.

"Leave me, Allun the baker. I am sick of your foolish face," hissed Sheba.

"I have also seen enough of yours," answered Allun, with a grim smile. "But I do not choose to leave my friend Rowan alone with you."

Sheba sneered at him, and turned in her chair to face Rowan. "So—we are to have a gathering," she said, baring her long brown teeth in a horrible grin. "Your companions—those who lurk outside—must join us, then. I have a fancy to see them face to face."

Rowan hesitated.

Sheba's grin disappeared. "Fetch them!" she thundered.

Rowan went back outside and beckoned to Zeel and Perlain. "She wants you, and I am sure she will not speak to me unless you come," he whispered to them. "But once you are inside, say nothing. Do not be tempted to—"

"Wise advice," croaked Sheba's voice from inside the hut. "Do not be tempted to match wits with me. Show yourselves!"

Zeel, brows drawn together in a frown, and Perlain, expressionless as only a Maris could be, followed Rowan into the dim little room.

"Ah! Now the gathering is complete," said Sheba, looking her new visitors up and down. "I had a half-breed clown and a Rin weakling turned hero. Now, to join them, a fishman out of water and a Zebak who pretends to be a Traveler. What a fine collection of oddities." She laughed heartily, slapping at her knees so that dust and ash flew into the thick air around her chair.

Rowan heard Zeel draw a quick breath of anger and saw Perlain glance at her and then veil his eyes. But they both kept silence. Allun, unfortunately, could not.

"You are forgetting to include yourself, good lady," he said loudly. "The greatest oddity of all."

Sheba abruptly stopped laughing. "I forget nothing, clown," she growled warningly. "And you would be wise to remember it."

There was a short, unpleasant silence. Then Sheba turned again to Rowan.

"Now, what gift have you brought for old Sheba, Rowan of the Bukshah?" she croaked. "What do you have to trade for the knowledge you seek? The knowledge only I can give you? Come closer." She smiled horribly.

"Beware, Rowan," muttered Allun. "She spits like a cat, but more unpleasantly."

Rowan moved farther into the room, his heart sinking. He had completely forgotten that Sheba would expect a gift. Allun had brought her honey cakes, sweet buns, and a bowl of fruits from the abandoned feast. Rowan could see them in a basket by the chair. Desperately he felt in his pockets, hoping to find something, anything, he could offer her.

She watched him in silence, waiting.

"I—I am sorry," he said at last. "I have nothing to trade just now. But what I ask is—is very important. I beg you to help me. If you do, I will make sure you are repaid."

"So." Sheba grinned, her eyes shining red in the firelight. "You will make sure, will you? And how, my little hero, will you do that, when you are in chains in the land of the Zebak?"

Rowan heard Allun's muffled gasp beside him, but

he did not turn to him or look at Perlain and Zeel standing by the door. He concentrated all his will on Sheba.

"I will write a note, asking my mother to make my promise good," he said. "She will do it."

"And will you give me whatever I ask?" demanded Sheba.

Rowan thought quickly. He knew she was trying to trap him. "I will give you what you ask if it is within my power to give," he said at last. "And if the giving hurts no other person."

He watched Sheba closely, but the old woman showed neither disappointment nor triumph. She just nodded. "Write, then," she said. "The pen is beside you."

Rowan looked and saw a pen, some ink, and a sheet of paper lying on a small table at Sheba's elbow. Realizing at once that she had planned this from the beginning, he knelt beside the table and picked up the pen with a feeling of dread.

"Rowan, do not trust her," Perlain warned.

Sheba darted him a black look. "Silence, fish-man!" she ordered.

But Rowan had put the pen down. "Before I write, give me the help you have promised, Sheba," he said, trying to keep his voice steady.

She grinned at him. "You have grown crafty and

bold, skinny rabbit. Crafty like your fishy friend. Bold like the pale-eyed Zebak girl. But what is to stop you running away, once I have given what I have to give and told what I have to tell?"

Rowan kept silence and looked down at the paper. He felt Sheba's eyes burning into his head, but he did not look up. He knew that if he did, he would not be able to hold firm.

A long minute passed. Then Rowan heard a sigh and a rustling sound, as though the old woman was moving in her chair.

"Very well," Sheba said.

Rowan looked up and saw that she was holding something out to him. It was a small, thin package, wrapped in oiled cloth and tied with a cord of faded, braided silk. He took it, his heart thudding with excitement. The wrapping cloth was thick, and smelled strongly of the fire, of ash, and of bitter herbs. He could not guess what might be inside. He began to pull at the cord, but the knots would not loosen.

"Only when you reach the land you seek will it open," muttered Sheba. "Its contents are for use when you really need them. When you have no hope. Till then, keep it well, for it is precious."

Rowan slipped the package inside his shirt, his fingers trembling.

"I have given what I have to give," said Sheba sullenly. "What I have to tell will be told after you have done your part. Now write."

Rowan dipped the pen in the ink and wrote. *Mother, I owe the wise woman Sheba a debt. She is to have—*

He stopped and looked up, the pen still poised over the paper. Sheba's eyes were gleaming. Her hands rubbed together, making a dry, rasping sound.

"What is it you want?" Rowan whispered.

"My price is small," said Sheba. "It is the black calf, born to the bukshah herd in spring."

Rowan went cold. The bukshah were loving and took comfort in each other's company. The thought of the little black calf being made to spend its life here alone, away from the open fields, away from its mother and its friends, was heartbreaking.

"The calf is too—too young to leave its mother," he stammered.

A slow grin spread over Sheba's face once more. "I will wait. For a while, as it happens, I will be much occupied, with no time for it."

"Why do you want it?" Rowan managed to ask.

"Because it takes my fancy." Sheba swung round to face him, and her grin broadened. "Because it is an oddity. Apart from the herd. Like me." She leaned forward, her greasy hair swinging around her face. "Like your friends here. And like you, Rowan of the Bukshah."

The words struck the most tender place in Rowan's mind and clung there, stinging like fiery sparks. He looked down again at the pen.

"Perhaps you care more for the beast's freedom than for your sister's," sneered Sheba. "If so, give me back my gift, and stop wasting my time."

Rowan knew he had to do what she asked. He wrote with a heavy heart, then stood up and held out the note. Sheba snatched it, studied it carefully with narrowed eyes, then nodded, satisfied.

"Good," she said, folding the paper and stuffing it under the cushion of her chair. "So—the time has come." She turned to Perlain, Allun, and Zeel. "Leave us," she said abruptly.

"I am comfortable here." Allun smiled.

Sheba's eyes glittered red.

"Please go," Rowan begged.

Zeel and Perlain exchanged glances. Zeel nodded, took Allun's arm and tugged at it. Perlain pushed the door open, and together he and Zeel managed to persuade Allun outside. The door closed behind them, and the latch fell with a click.

The little room seemed empty without them. Rowan stood by Sheba's chair, feeling very alone.

5 ∽ THE RHYME

 Taking no notice of Rowan, Sheba bent, picked up a handful of tiny sticks from the box beside her chair, and threw them onto the fire. They blazed up instantly, red and green flames dancing on the blackened wood. Misshapen shadows leaped like evil spirits about the room. Rowan's skin began to prickle with fear.

"Hold out your hand!" Sheba ordered suddenly.

Hesitantly, Rowan stretched out his right hand and the old woman seized his wrist. She gripped it tightly, her pointed nails digging into his flesh. He took a sharp breath and looked up. His eyes were caught and held by hers. They were strangely mocking and deep, so deep. He could not look away.

"Now we will see which of us is stronger," Sheba

droned in an altered voice. Her eyes grew deeper still, drawing him in. It was as though he was falling into them, plunging down, down. . . .

Then, dimly, as if from far away, he heard Sheba cackling. He struggled, blinked, and the spell was broken. She was laughing in his face, still gripping his wrist.

"So." She grinned. With astonishing strength, she dragged his hand toward the fire. The flames flickered higher, licking at Rowan's fingers like greedy tongues, scorching and burning.

With a cry he struggled to pull away, but Sheba's grip was as hard as stone and she was no longer listening to him. Her head was flung back, her eyes were closed, and she was mumbling to herself, swaying slightly from side to side. The fire burned higher, higher—she began to speak. The words came to Rowan through a haze of searing pain:

> *Five strange fingers form fate's hand,*
> *Each plays its part at fate's command.*
> *The fiery blaze the answer keeps.*
> *And till its time each secret sleeps.*
> *When pain is truth and truth is pain,*
> *The painted shadows live again.*
> *Five leave, but five do not return.*
> *Vain hope and pride in terror burn.*

Sheba's eyes opened, and Rowan felt her grip loosen. He wrenched himself away from her and stumbled back from the fire, cradling his injured hand against his chest, sobbing with pain and shock. He could hear banging on the door, and Allun and Zeel shouting. But the door was sealed against them.

Sheba was lying back in her chair as if exhausted, but still she found the strength to laugh. "Oh, my little hero," she jeered, "did you not like old Sheba's lesson? Here is another."

The pain rose in a great wave, unbearable. And then, suddenly, it disappeared as if it had never been.

Bewildered and shaking, Rowan looked down. Instead of being burned and blistered as he had expected, his hand was smooth and unmarked. He stared at it, astounded.

"Not all is as it seems," croaked Sheba. "Now—be off with you, before your foolish friends injure themselves by beating at my door."

Rowan felt anger rise in him. It burned in his chest, searing hot, like the fire that had burned his hand. He fought it down with all his strength.

"Allun, Zeel," he shouted toward the door. "Wait!"

The banging stopped, and he faced Sheba once

more. "You have not yet told me what I need to know," he said and wondered at the calmness of his voice.

She shrugged. "I have told you what I can, which is all I promised. You have the words. Remember them."

"They are not enough!" Rowan exclaimed. "You have not told me where I must go in the land of the Zebak, and what I must do, to save Annad."

"How could I tell you that, Rowan of the Bukshah?" Sheba yawned. "How could I know? The land of the Zebak is far away. Too far—even for me." Her eyes closed.

"But—you did not tell me this before!" Angry tears stung Rowan's eyes. He dashed them away furiously.

Sheba's thin mouth curved into a smile. "You . . . did not ask," she murmured.

"You tricked me!" Rowan started toward her, his hands reaching out to shake her, make her speak to him further. But the fire blazed up with a fierce crackling as he took the first step, and his right hand began to sting and burn.

He jumped back with a gasp, cradling his hand as the pain rose to an agonizing peak and then faded away. He did not dare approach Sheba again. He stood helplessly in the center of the room, staring at her with loathing. She lay motionless in her chair, breathing deeply. She was asleep, and he knew she would not wake.

When Rowan stepped outside the hut, he was first amazed, then horrified, to see that it was nearly dark. He looked wildly around, hardly able to believe his eyes. The sun had been high in the sky when first he crossed the clearing to listen at Sheba's door. How could so much time have passed?

Then he remembered the fire flickering red and green, and Sheba's fingers tightening on his wrist. And her eyes—deep, mocking . . .

The clearing was deserted. He jumped as two shadows moved under the orchard trees, then relaxed when he saw it was only Allun and Zeel, coming to meet him.

"What did the witch do to you?" Zeel demanded furiously.

Allun's face was drawn. "You were in the hut for so long! Then we heard you cry out in pain—great pain."

"It was nothing," Rowan said. But he could not stop himself from shuddering at the memory of what had happened.

"It was because I teased her that she turned on

you," muttered Allun. "Because I could not keep my idiot tongue safely behind my teeth."

Rowan shook his head. "It is not your fault. She tormented you, angered you, to make you do it. I should not have stayed. She tricked me. She enchanted me to make me stay far longer than I intended. And then she told me little."

And what she told me, I would rather not have known, he thought.

"Tell us," Allun urged.

Reluctantly, Rowan repeated the rhyme. With every word his hand throbbed with remembered pain.

Allun and Zeel listened intently, but when Rowan's voice trailed off, they looked at each other in bewilderment.

"All this talk of fire and burning is not pleasant," said Allun. "And these painted shadows that are going to live again—what are they?"

"I do not know." Rowan sighed. "I do not understand any of it."

He rubbed his eyes, trying to clear his mind, then suddenly realized that someone was missing. "Where is Perlain?" he asked urgently. "We must go."

"Perlain left for Maris, with Tor, long ago," said Allun. He smiled tiredly and held up his hand as

Rowan's eyes filled with panic. "No, do not fear. He has not abandoned you."

"Ogden was here, waiting for us, when we came out of the hut," Zeel explained. "He said he believed that you would be with Sheba for some time, and that Perlain should not wait."

Rowan shook his head desperately.

Zeel touched his shoulder with cool fingers, calming him. "Ogden's plan will save much time," she told him. "I am to take you directly to the coast from here, following the way the creature flew. Meanwhile, Perlain will be bringing the boat from Maris."

"But—the cliffs—the rocks!" exclaimed Rowan, confused. "Maris is the only safe landing place on the coast. That is why the Zebak have never come—"

"All that has been thought of, Rowan," said Allun gently. "Ogden has power over the wind, remember, Perlain's boat will wait out at sea, in the calmer water. Zeel and Mithren, who has the white kite, will fly us there from the land."

Rowan nodded, taking it in. Much had happened, it seemed, while he was with Sheba. His friends had been thinking and planning for him.

He blinked, suddenly focusing on something Allun had said. "*Us?*" he exclaimed. "Allun, you said, 'Fly *us*.'"

"Oh, yes," Allun said carelessly. "I am curious to see what is inside Sheba's little package. Sadly, it cannot be opened until you reach the land of the Zebak. So I have decided that I simply must go with you."

6 ∝ INTO THE DARK

All the way to the Travelers' camp, Rowan tried to persuade Allun to change his mind. But Allun would not listen. He swung along, laughing and joking, as though he really *was* happy to go into terrible danger just to find out what was in Sheba's package.

"I have inherited my father's Traveler curiosity, Rowan," he said. "Travelers feel they must know everything. And half-Travelers are no different, it seems. What is more, I cannot resist the chance to soar the wind with a kite once again."

He laughed slyly. "Perlain felt differently," he said. "'I cannot understand it,' I said to him. 'There is nothing I love better than flying.' But he was green and shaking at the very thought."

Zeel strode beside them, saying nothing. Finally,

when they had reached the camp and were moving to where Ogden waited for them, she spoke.

"Do you not *want* company on this quest, Rowan of the Bukshah?" she asked bluntly. "Did the witch tell you that you must go to the land of the Zebak alone, if you are to succeed?"

Rowan swallowed, looking down at his feet. "No," he said reluctantly. "But—it was *my* fault that my sister was lost. To try to find her is *my* idea—an idea that all in Rin will think is folly. I—do not wish any other person to be in danger because of me."

Zeel nodded and stopped. She turned to Allun. "So," she said. "Stop your foolishness. Stop hiding your softness like a snail hiding in its shell. Explain your real reason for going on this quest."

Allun's easy smile wavered, then disappeared, leaving his lean face sad and serious. "I will not be in danger because of you, Rowan," he said quietly. "I *always* intended to go after the beast. Why do you imagine I visited Sheba's hut? For the same reason as you did—to try to gain advice and guidance for the journey."

He saw Rowan stare at him in amazement, and shrugged. "I was only partly joking about the Travelers' need to know. I have it, strongly. But in me it joins with the Rin love of home, and a safe, settled life. I cannot simply wait here, preparing to defend the valley. I must know what the Zebak are planning. How can we raise children if we are always in fear that they will be snatched away from us? Come. Ogden is waiting."

He began to walk again, moving very quickly toward the place where Ogden stood. Mithren was there, too, Rowan noticed now. His white kite was over his shoulder. He was ready.

With Zeel by his side, Rowan hurried after Allun.

"He is thinking of his own children," Zeel murmured. "The children he will have one day, if he marries Marlie the weaver."

Rowan nodded slowly. Shocked, guilty and grieved, focused on Annad, he had not thought of the future. But now he saw that Allun was right. After this day, the Rin valley could no longer be thought of as a safe, protected place. The arching sky itself was now an open gate through which, at any time, terror might come.

They flew into the dark, sped by the wind that Ogden had summoned. It seemed to Rowan, as the lights of Rin winked and faded away beneath him, that the dark was swallowing them up.

He had left carrying nothing but Sheba's small package, the burning memory of her mysterious words and a bitter knowledge of the price he had

paid for them. The only farewell he had given was
to Star. The only word he had left for his mother
was a scribbled note, which Ogden had promised
to deliver.

It was as though he had cut himself adrift from
everything he knew and loved and was lost in a
rushing black sea that had no ending.

Every now and then, out of the corner of his eye,
he caught sight of a glimmer of white. He knew it
was the Traveler Mithren's kite, and that Allun was
flying with it, bound to Mithren by cords of silk, as
Rowan was bound to Zeel. But Mithren and Allun
were hidden by the dark. Only the kite sail, wheeling and dipping in and out of view, was proof that
Rowan and Zeel were not alone.

They flew for hours, and Rowan could only trust
that Zeel knew where they were and was steering in
the right direction. The stars were guiding her, he
knew that. But to him the stars were just chilly white
points in the sky, and all of them looked the same.

He found himself drifting to sleep, then waking
with a start. Each time he woke, he thought for an
instant that he had been living in a nightmare and
that now he was safe in his bed at home. Then he
would open his eyes to the black sky, and feel the
cool wind beating against his face, and realize that
this was no dream.

Finally, confused and fearful, he would remember Sheba's words. He had tried not to think of them, but he could not forget them. They seemed to flame red in his mind, colored by the memory of burning pain.

> *Five strange fingers form fate's hand,*
> *Each plays its part at fate's command.*
> *The fiery blaze the answer keeps,*
> *And till its time each secret sleeps.*
> *When pain is truth and truth is pain,*
> *The painted shadows live again.*
> *Five leave, but five do not return.*
> *Vain hope and pride in terror burn.*

What could the rhyme mean? He knew from experience that Sheba's prophecies were to be taken seriously, however mysterious they seemed. But this . . .

Five strange fingers . . .

"Rowan, we are passing the coast," Zeel shouted to him above the wind. "Look down."

Rowan looked and saw. He saw the still blackness of earth disappear and the moving blackness of water take its place. He saw white foam flying upward as dark water dashed against darker cliffs. Here, in this place he had never seen before, his land ended, and strangeness began.

Now they were leaving the cliffs behind and flying over the sea. At first the water below them boiled and frothed around huge hidden rocks, surging angrily in many different directions. Gradually, though, it deepened and calmed as they flew on, on, far out of sight of land.

And only then did Rowan feel a pang of fear. Soon, surely, Ogden's power over the wind would falter. If the wind were to drop, if the kite were to fall, he and Zeel would plunge together into that dark, mysterious water where serpents coiled, hunting for prey. Tied together, the silk of the kite swirling and twisting around them, how could they keep afloat? He was a weak swimmer in any case, and—his stomach tightened as he remembered—Travelers did not swim at all. That was why Allun—

Allun! Rowan realized that he had not seen the white glimmer of Mithren's kite since they crossed the coastline. In panic he twisted left and right, desperately searching the darkness. The kite slowed and swayed.

"Rowan! They are safe behind us. Be still!" Zeel shouted, her voice thin and torn by the wind. "Look ahead!"

She shifted her weight, steadied the kite, and steered it on, toward the tiny light that her sharp eyes had seen long ago, and that now even Rowan saw for himself. It was the light of Perlain's boat riding the dark sea, waiting for them.

Alone, Zeel would have settled on the boat's rocking deck as easily and lightly as she would have landed on the grass of a green field. But Rowan, stiff and clumsy from the long flight, stumbled as his feet touched the smooth boards. He fell heavily, dragging Zeel down with him.

"I—I am sorry," he stammered. He tried to rise, found that his legs would not support him, and fell back. The boat tilted and rolled.

Perlain, sure-footed, padded toward them. He crouched to steady Rowan as Zeel unclipped the ties that bound them together.

Zeel laughed as finally she stood up, gathering the folds of the yellow kite from behind her and tossing them over her shoulder. She looked up into the blackness of the sky. Her eyes were shining with excitement.

"Back," she ordered. "Mithren is coming in with Allun. Give him room."

With Perlain's help, Rowan scrambled awkwardly away from the landing place, finally reaching the mast of the boat. He clung to it gratefully, and at last managed to haul himself to his feet. He heard Zeel give a shout and quickly turned to look.

She was standing in the middle of the deck, staring upward. The white sail of Mithren's kite hovered high above her, hardly moving. Rowan caught his breath. What was wrong?

"Why is Mithren not landing?" he asked Perlain anxiously. "Why—?"

At that moment there was a call from the kite. Zeel raised her arms and with a shock Rowan saw a body falling from below the white sail. Or . . . not falling, but drifting downward through the darkness. He watched, open-mouthed, as the figure sank farther and at last moved into the light that streamed upward from the boat.

It was Allun, white-faced but determined. He was suspended on a thin cord, swinging from it like a spider on a strand of silk. Zeel was waiting for him, arms still upraised. She caught him around the waist as soon as he was within reach, and held him fast.

"It is well!" she called, looking up at the hovering kite. Immediately the tightly stretched cord slackened as, far above, Mithren cut it free. It dropped lightly to the deck and Zeel staggered as she took Allun's full weight. He slipped from her grasp and fell, stumbling and rolling as Rowan had done, as soon as his feet touched the boards.

Perlain rushed to help him, but Zeel paid no attention. She was still looking up.

"Mithren, I will see you again!" she shouted, waving.

"I will see you again, Zeel," came the faint answering cry. The white sail billowed, dipped, and began moving away, turning in a great circle and then speeding off into the darkness.

Still clinging to the mast, Rowan stared at Zeel, his eyes full of questions. She returned his gaze without speaking.

"Does Mithren not want to rest here before returning?" he asked.

She shook her head. "He must get back within the circle of Ogden's power as soon as he can," she said. "The wind out here is changeable and dangerous."

"But you—what of you?" demanded Rowan. He turned to Perlain, standing silent behind him. "And what of Perlain?"

"We are where we want to be," said Perlain quietly.

"We have decided that this quest is not yours or Allun's alone," Zeel added. "It is ours also. We are coming with you."

Rowan's heart gave a great leap.

Allun smiled brightly, though his face was still as pale as death. "A collection of oddities we may be," he said. "But it seems that fate has decided that we are to do its work."

Five strange fingers form fate's hand . . .

Rowan made a small sound and clutched his right hand. It was throbbing and burning as the words echoed in his mind.

Zeel glanced at him and lifted her chin. "Fate has decided nothing. We have decided for ourselves. And we are four, not five. Do not fear, Rowan. The rhyme cannot mean us."

"Unless"—Rowan wet his dry lips—"there is another."

The boat rocked dangerously, and he clung to the mast to stop himself from falling.

"The tide is turning," he heard Perlain's flat voice say. "And the wind is rising. We must put up the sails and move from here. Even now we could be swept into shore and smashed on the rocks. There is no time to lose."

7 ∾ THE TEMPEST

Perlain had brought three vests made of cork. One for Allun, one for Zeel, and one for Rowan.

"They float in the sea. Our people use them when they have been injured," he explained. "When they have lost the use of their arms or legs and cannot swim safely in rough water."

"I have perfect use of my arms and legs. And I can swim!" snapped Zeel, looking at the thick, clumsy brown garment in disgust. "The Zebak learn to swim before they learn to walk. How else do you think I survived long enough to be washed up alive on the coast, where Ogden found me?"

Perlain smiled slightly. "Perhaps you can swim," he said. "But not like a Maris. And by the appearance of the waves and the smell of the wind, I fear you may need to swim like a Maris before our journey is over."

Allun and Rowan were already tying on their vests gratefully. After a moment's hesitation, Zeel did the same. Perlain nodded with satisfaction, then turned his attention to the sails.

The wind rose higher and the sails filled. For many hours the boat seemed to fly over the tops of the waves, speeding as fast and as easily as a Traveler's kite through the air. They took turns resting, though only Perlain seemed actually to sleep. The others lay awake, turning uncomfortably in the hard cork vests, disturbed instead of lulled by the endless movement of the boat.

Dawn came at last, but cloud veiled the sun and the sea was gray, with swelling waves. Perlain, Rowan, and Zeel nibbled dried fish and drank water. Allun took only water. His face was greenish white. Plainly he felt very ill, and as the morning wore on he became worse and worse. Finally he could do nothing but lie, groaning, at the bottom of the boat, covered in a blanket.

Rowan bent over him, his face creased in concern.

"I am dying, Rowan," moaned Allun.

"No, you are not, my friend," said Perlain calmly,

looking down from his place at the helm. "As I have told you many times, land-bound creatures often suffer this sickness at sea. It is the movement of the boat, they say."

He allowed himself a small smile as he turned away to check one of the ropes. "I cannot understand it," Rowan heard him murmur. "There is nothing I love better than sailing."

As morning became afternoon, Allun slowly began to feel better. By evening he was able to get up and even eat a little.

"Never again will I make fun of you for being afraid of flying," he promised Perlain, "if you will swear never to bring me to sea again."

But by this time Perlain was not in the mood for smiling. The bad weather he had felt brewing was almost upon them. The clouds, dark gray and angry looking, tumbled and raced low above their heads. The wind was blowing harder. The dark, heaving water was being whipped into sharp points tipped with white foam.

And at last the full force of the storm struck them. Rain pelted down, the boat heaved and tossed in the great waves, and the sails were torn by wind that seemed to have no ending and no mercy.

As they plunged on into the black night, the wind howling around them and the waves beating

against the frail sides of the boat, Rowan realized
that his plan to make this journey alone had been
more than foolishness. It had been insanity.

He could never have kept the boat afloat in this
raging sea. Nor could Allun have helped him—or
Zeel, whatever her determination and courage. It
was Perlain, and Perlain only, who could do it.

Perlain had been born to the sea, and he knew it
as none of his companions could ever do. Without
Perlain's small webbed hand on the tiller, and Perlain's urgent voice telling them which rope to pull,
which way to put their weight, which sail to raise or
lower, they would all have perished within hours.

But it was Perlain, the only one of them who
truly understood the sea's power, who was most
afraid. And it was he who warned them, after hours
of fighting the storm, that they were in terrible
danger.

"The mast will not hold," he shouted above the
roaring of the wind. "It is strained beyond bearing.
We are taking in water. And the gale is growing
stronger. We must prepare—"

"For a swim?" Allun's lean face tightened. He was
wet through. The muscles of his arms strained
against the ropes he held as he and Zeel leaned
back over the side of the boat, using their weight to
keep it upright.

"Yes," shouted Perlain. "But do not despair. The sea is shallower here than before—I can feel it. The wind has driven us fast and hard. I believe we are not far from shore—though not where I intended."

"Where then?" called Zeel.

Before Perlain could answer, there was a huge gust of wind and a terrible, groaning crack as the mast snapped. With a cry he leaped clear as the wooden pole tilted and crashed down, crushing the tiller and smashing the side of the boat. Then a great wave swept over the deck, and where Perlain had stood there was nothing but hissing, swirling water.

"Perlain!" Rowan screamed. But even as he shouted, he felt the boat rolling and tilting, the deck sliding out from under his feet. And before he could think or cry out again, he was gasping and struggling in the cold black sea.

Waves crashed around him. Blinded and deafened by the pounding water, he tossed helplessly, one minute overwhelmed by the tide, the next minute forced to the surface again by the cork vest, choking and fighting for air.

"Allun!" he called. "Zeel! Perlain!" But he could hear nothing. Nothing but the roaring of the gale and the crashing of the waves and the awful splintering, smashing sound of the boat breaking up.

Something reared out of the blackness beside him. Serpent! In his terror and confusion Rowan lashed out, shouting, choking as saltwater rushed into his mouth and nose. He struggled blindly, his mind filled with the terrible picture of a slimy, twisting body, dripping jaws, needle-sharp teeth.

Then his hand hit rough hardness, and he realized that the object beside him was not a serpent at all. It was a large piece of wood that had floated clear of the smashed boat. He clutched at it, using his last strength to haul himself partly onto it so that his head and chest rested on its hard surface.

He could do no more. Clinging to the wood, panting and trembling, tossed and blown like a piece of wreckage himself, he screwed his eyes shut. Annad, I am sorry, he thought. Then he let the waves take him where they would.

"Rowan! Rowan!"

The voice was calling from a long way off. Rowan did not want to answer it. He wanted to stay where he was, lulled by soft hissing and rippling sounds, dozing in this pleasant half-sleep where nothing was real and there was nothing to be feared. But now a hand was shaking his shoulder and the voice was louder, louder. . . .

He frowned, mumbled, and opened his eyes.

They stung and watered, and at first he could see nothing but darkness.

"Take heart! He is with us!" the voice called.

There were faint, hoarse cheers from somewhere nearby.

Gradually Rowan's vision cleared, and through the watery dimness he saw a face he knew, bending close to his.

Perlain.

Rowan tried to speak, but his throat was dry and felt scratched and torn. He pressed his hand to his neck, swallowed, and tried again. "Perlain!" he croaked. "I thought you were drowned."

Perlain smiled and shook his head. "I am not so easily disposed of, my friend," he said. "But I have thought *you* were drowned for the past hour. And now, like a miracle, the tide has brought you in, draped like a piece of draggled weed over some planks of my poor boat."

"Allun?" croaked Rowan. "Zeel?"

"They are both here," Perlain said. "They are resting, feeling sorry for themselves. Like you, they have swallowed a lot of saltwater, and it has not agreed with them." He looked around, a little uneasily. "Do you feel strong enough to move now?" he asked politely. "Serpents often choose to hunt close to shore. Especially after a storm, when there may be injured prey floundering in the shallows."

Only then did Rowan realize that he was lying in shallow water and that Perlain was holding his head up and away from the small waves that were bubbling and hissing around him. Painfully he managed to stand up. Then, leaning on the Maris man's shoulder, he waded with him to the shore.

Allun and Zeel were sprawled against a small hillock of sand not far away. Both were pale, wet, and shivering, but both grinned with pleasure when they saw Rowan.

"We are a fine party of heroes," Allun joked through chattering teeth. "Half drowned, half frozen, half dead with tiredness and sick to our stomachs through drinking half the ocean. Not to mention that all our supplies are feeding the fish."

"At least we are alive," said Zeel as Rowan slumped down beside her. "The storm is over. I still have my flint, to start a fire. I have rope, and my kite, too. Perlain has his knife and has saved one water bag. And"—she looked hopefully at the Maris man—"surely we are somewhere *near* where we had intended to be?"

Perlain returned her gaze, hesitating. The corners of his mouth were tight, and when he spoke his voice sounded strained and odd. "Not so near. But we are in the territory of the Zebak, certainly. I think this is a place I have seen from far offshore in the past. If it is, we are safe for now, but . . ." His voice trailed away.

"But what, Perlain?" asked Rowan.

Perlain shook his head, turned away, and started picking up sticks of driftwood from the sand. "It is nothing. And in any case I cannot tell if I am right until dawn."

For a few moments he remained silent, then he cleared his throat and turned back to them, smiling. "For now, the most urgent task is to light a fire. You are all very cold and wet, and if you rest like this you will be ill. I know how weak and tender you warm-blooded creatures are."

At that, Zeel and Allun laughed and staggered to their feet to help him. They told Rowan to lie where he was, and indeed he had little choice. He was still dizzy and sick, and his chest ached every time he drew breath.

Zeel started a tiny blaze with dried grass and a spark struck from the flint she carried, then fed small twigs into the flames. The fire grew brighter, then stronger still as heavier pieces of wood were added.

The flickering light, the warmth and the pleasant crackling were comforting, and Rowan began to feel more himself. But as his mind cleared, grim thoughts began to torment him.

The boat was wrecked. None of his companions had spoken of what this meant, but it must be in all their minds. Whatever the result of their quest, there was no easy way home for them now.

And what of Annad? While they lay here on this strange shore, she was at the mercy of the Zebak. Alone, imprisoned, perhaps injured and in pain . . .

He pushed the thoughts away and sat up. He realized he was still wearing the cork vest. It had saved his life, but it was uncomfortable now. He fumbled at its ties, managed to undo them, and began to pull the vest off.

As he did so, he felt Sheba's package beneath his shirt. His heart thudded. He had completely forgotten about it. The storm, the wreck of the boat, his fear for his companions, and his own fight for life had driven it from his mind.

With trembling fingers he pulled it from its hiding place.

8 ∽ THE HAND OF FATE

 The bundle was sodden—the oilcloth had not been able to withstand its long soaking in the sea.

"Rowan! Sheba's gift—how could I have forgotten?" exclaimed Allun, sitting down beside him. "Quickly, open it! It may be the only thing that will help us now."

"It is wet through." Zeel frowned. "Whatever is inside may be spoiled."

Rowan fumbled with the braided cord that tied the package. This time the knots loosened easily. He pulled away the cord and slowly began to unwrap the oilcloth. He was afraid of what he might find inside. If the contents were ruined, he could not bear it. He had promised Sheba the black bukshah calf in return for this package, and on it he had pinned all his hopes.

The cloth was folded and rolled over many, many times. Most of the thickness of the package was due to that. There was plainly much less inside it than Rowan had believed.

"Whatever she has given us, she has protected it well," said Allun doubtfully.

"Almost too well for sense, one might think," added Perlain, his face expressionless.

His heart beating fast, Rowan pulled away the last of the wrapping cloth, finally revealing what was inside.

A piece of grimy metal. A small bundle of the pale grass that grew outside Sheba's hut. And a few twigs.

He stared in disbelief. The disappointment was so bitter that it brought stinging tears to his eyes.

"What is this?" hissed Zeel.

Perlain's face was stern. "What I have feared. The witch has played a trick—to repay me for warning Rowan not to trust her, and to repay him for listening to me. He told her he would not write down his promise to her until she had passed over her part of the bargain."

"She gave you some sticks from her fire basket, Rowan. With some grass and a piece of old iron added for weight," muttered Allun in disgust. "All nicely wrapped in cloth that would disguise them.

No wonder she insisted you did not unwrap the package until you were far from home."

Zeel gritted her teeth. "No doubt she believes we will not return, and so she is safe."

"I am sorry," said Rowan in a low voice.

"Do not be," said Allun. "Sheba must have planned to deceive you all along. The package was ready and waiting for her to pass to you, remember. This is not your fault, or Perlain's—or even mine, for once."

He looked down at his hands. Plainly, despite his lighthearted words, he was dismayed by what had happened. Zeel and Perlain, too, were silent, staring into the fire. Rowan knew that the same thoughts were in all their minds: One flint. One water bag. A piece of rope. A knife. No way to return home. And soon it will be dawn. Where are we to go? What are we to do?

"There is still the rhyme," he murmured.

"But what does it mean?" Zeel demanded bitterly. "It is impossible to understand."

"Not at all. Sheba simply failed to count us properly," Allun replied, straight-faced. "I have been thinking about it, and I am certain that we are the fingers of fate's hand, even though we are only four. Zeel is the tall, straight middle finger. Perlain is the small, wriggling one at the end. I am the ring finger, good for nothing but decoration. And Rowan is the strong little thumb that makes us all behave as we should."

Even Perlain smiled at this, but his smile quickly faded. "Perhaps you are right," he said quietly. "And perhaps, then, this is another of Sheba's jokes, for the finger that is missing is the first finger. The pointer. The one that shows the way. And it is certain that this is the very one we need."

Zeel moved restlessly, then pulled a piece of burning wood from the fire and stood up. Soon she was climbing the sand dunes behind them, using the wood as a torch. After a moment Allun joined her. They were quickly swallowed by the darkness, but Rowan saw the flickering light climb to the top of the dunes and then move around as Zeel turned in all directions to peer at the land beyond.

"Do not go out of sight," Perlain called. "Do not leave the shore!"

"Perlain," said Rowan in a low voice, "what is this place? Why are you afraid of it? Tell me."

Perlain shifted uncomfortably. "I think—that we are at the edge of what I have heard called the Wastelands," he said at last. "About it I know nothing, except that it is said to be vast and barren. It is Zebak territory, but no Zebak ventures into the Wastelands. It is a forbidden place."

"Why?" Rowan asked.

Perlain turned his head away. "I do not know," he mumbled.

He looked up and saw Zeel and Allun returning. Their torch had burned down to a dull glow. "Say nothing to them yet, Rowan," he whispered. "Perhaps I am wrong about where we are. I hope that I am."

Zeel and Allun flung themselves down in front of the fire again.

"There is a glow, very faint and far away, on what may be the horizon," Zeel reported, throwing her smoldering torch back into the fire. "We could hear some shrieks and scratching noises. But that is all. The blackness is almost complete. Even the trees do not show against the sky. I had hoped to launch the kite and mark out our course, but we will have to wait till dawn."

"As you say," murmured Perlain. "Sunrise will be the test."

There was an uncomfortable silence, broken only by the sound of the waves breaking on the sand and the crackling of the fire.

Rowan tossed one of the sticks from the unwrapped package into the flames, but it was still too wet to burn. It steamed sulkily and he stared at it, shaking his head. Sheba's gift, on which he had so foolishly depended, was not useful even for burning. How could he have been taken in by her tricks? How could he have trusted her?

Because she has always, in the end, proved worthy of trust.

The thought drifted into his mind, and clung there.

He looked at the piece of metal, still lying with the four remaining twigs and the pale grass on the oilcloth in his lap. He picked it up and held it to the light. It was not just scrap metal, or part of the old fire grate, as he had first thought. It was dirty and dull, and it was heavy, but it was . . . a medallion of some sort.

Hope flickered in his heart. He rubbed at the medallion with his shirt. As dirt and soot came away from the dull surface he could see that it was decorated and that a small metal loop was fixed to one end. It was meant to be worn on a chain—around the neck, no doubt.

"It could be that this is more useful than it appears," he said hesitantly, holding it up so that the others could see it.

Allun held out his hand, and Rowan gave the medallion to him. But he did it reluctantly. Suddenly he had become aware that he did not want to let it go. He watched jealously as it was passed around.

"Perhaps it is a charm," said Zeel, looking at it curiously. "Perhaps it will bring us good fortune." She passed it to Perlain and went back to staring into the fire, her brow furrowed in thought.

"It has not been particularly lucky for us up till now," said Perlain, handing the medallion back to Rowan. "But we shall see."

Rowan held the smooth piece of metal tightly for a moment, weighing it in his hand. Was it something? Or nothing? He could not tell. But Sheba had said the package was precious. And the medallion was the only possibly precious thing in it.

On a sudden impulse, he picked up the braided silk cord that had fastened the package and threaded it through the small metal loop. Working quickly, he tied the ends of the cord together and slipped it around his neck so that the medallion hung low on his chest, hidden by his shirt.

When this had been done, he felt strangely relieved. Now that the medallion was safe, protected, and hidden from sight once more, it was as though a great weight had been taken from his mind.

But why? he asked himself. Even if it is some magic charm, why keep it a secret? And if it is just an ornament, with no meaning. . . . He smiled at himself, shaking his head at his own foolishness.

"Rowan!"

At first he did not recognize the voice as Zeel's. It was so low, so choked. He looked up, startled. Zeel was moving back from the fire, pointing into the flames. Her eyes were wide and frightened.

Rowan looked into the blaze. The damp stick he had thrown there had dried out and caught alight. Green flames were dancing along its length. The whole fire was alive with green light, darting here and there, mixing with the orange and red.

He stared, fascinated. He heard the exclamations of Allun and Perlain as they, too, saw what was happening, but he could not look away. There was a shape growing in the midst of the flames. A face. A face with red eyes, staring at him.

And there was a voice. It hissed in his brain like fire itself, and his right hand began to throb with pain as the words came to him:

> *The light that gleams at their back door*
> *Will guide you from the lonely shore,*
> *But dangers seek you as you go,*
> *One from above, one from below.*
> *One hides by night, one hides by day,*
> *And hard and stony is your way.*

The voice faded. The face disappeared. The green light began to die away. Rowan blinked and took a deep, shuddering breath. When he looked again, the fire was glowing red and orange. The stick was just a thin tube of fine white ash that crumbled as he watched.

He looked up and met the startled eyes of Perlain, Zeel, and Allun.

"What devilry is this?" whispered Zeel.

"It seems," Rowan said, trying to keep his voice steady, "that we have found the fifth member of our party. The pointing finger, the one who is to show us the way—is Sheba herself."

After Rowan had repeated the words that had come to him from the fire, the four companions sat for a moment in silence.

"This rhyme is clearer than the other," said Allun at last. "But I cannot say it is any more pleasing."

Zeel frowned. "The light we are to follow must be the glow we saw on the horizon. A light from the Zebak city, no doubt, for the rhyme speaks of 'their back door.' But the glow will not be visible to guide us by day."

"Then we should move on at once," Allun suggested eagerly. He jumped to his feet, but Perlain and Zeel both shook their heads.

"We cannot risk further disaster by plunging into the unknown with no supplies and no knowledge of what is ahead," said Zeel firmly. "There could be cliffs, deep holes, even water into which we could stumble. It is only a few hours till dawn. We should wait till then."

Perlain nodded agreement. "It will help no one if we all perish because we are unprepared. The rhyme says clearly that our way from here is to be hard. It also says that we are to face dangers both day and night, and they are to come from all around us, including the sky."

"The creature that carried Annad away attacked by day," Allun said. "And it came from the sky. It dropped like a thunderbolt. If there are more—if they patrol this place . . ."

Their voices seemed distant and echoing to Rowan. He still felt stunned by what he had seen in the fire, and Sheba's words had filled him with foreboding. But an overwhelming tiredness had settled over him like a heavy mist. It was pressing him down, down into sleep.

Struggling against it, he wrapped the remaining four sticks again and put the package away inside his shirt. But he yawned as he did so, and his eyes kept closing.

Perlain stood up. "The sky will soon lighten," he said. "I cannot soak because of the serpents, but I will lie on the wet sand for a time."

He stalked away, toward the sea.

Allun stared after him, frowning. "Something is worrying Perlain," he murmured.

"It would be strange if that were not so!" exclaimed Zeel. "We have much to think about."

"Well, if we are to stay here till dawn, I, for one, am going to think with my eyes closed, like Rowan," Allun said.

"You sleep," answered Zeel. "I will keep watch."

And Rowan heard no more.

It was bright day and already very warm when Rowan woke. He opened his eyes with a guilty start and sat up so quickly that his head swam.

He was alone by the cold ashes of the fire. There was the sound of waves softly breaking on the shore. The sky was a perfect blue bowl above his head.

He heard voices and looked around. Perlain, Allun, and Zeel were walking up from the sea. All of them were wet, and all were carrying dripping objects in their hands.

"Some of our supplies were washed to the shore during the night," Allun called as they grew nearer. "We have collected what we could."

Perlain reached Rowan first. "Do you feel refreshed?" he asked, bending to place a fish-skin bag and a sodden blanket on the sand.

Rowan nodded, deeply ashamed that he had slept so long—slept for even an hour while Annad was in such peril. He was ashamed, too, that he had slept while the others worked. And ashamed that they had let him do it, out of their kindness.

How tired I am of always being a burden, he thought suddenly. Others of my age in Rin are strong and can face any task. Why was I born such a weakling?

He turned away from Perlain, fighting down the pain he felt. Sheba was right. He was an oddity—a stranger in his herd like the black bukshah calf. He was prized by his people now for what he had done. But he would never be prized for what he *was*. His qualities were not those valued in Rin.

He knew that there had been other shy, gentle children born in the village over the past three hundred years. He had heard tales of them, which only showed how rare they were. Many had been keepers of the bukshah before him, because the great beasts were so easy to manage. Most had never married or had children of their own. They had spent their lives very much alone, with only the animals for company. Oddities. Never really understood or accepted.

"Are you unwell, my friend?"

Rowan looked up and found that Perlain was gazing at him in concern. He shook his head and managed to smile just as Allun and Zeel reached them.

"Two packets of dried fish," announced Allun as he and Zeel threw their wet burdens down beside Perlain's. "Another water bag. Some sort of speckled biscuit that seems to be so hard that even the sea has not melted it—or is it a piece of cork?"

"It is seaweed cake," Perlain answered calmly. "My people use it on long voyages. It is nourishing and light to carry. It is fortunate you found it. It will be useful—in the Wastelands."

With a sinking heart, Rowan realized that Perlain, Allun, and Zeel had already investigated the land beyond the shore. That was why they seemed so joking and so full of energy. They were keeping up their spirits, taking their minds off what was before them.

"You were right, then," he said to Perlain in a low voice.

Perlain nodded, avoiding his eyes.

Rowan saw Zeel and Allun glance at each other. There was something they were not telling him.

He stood up unsteadily and without looking back trudged up the hills of sand to the place where Zeel and Allun had stood the night before. Then at last the land beyond the dunes lay spread out before him, and dread filled his heart.

The sun glared down on a vast plain that stretched away on all sides as far as the eye could see. Rowan remembered Zeel complaining in the night that it was so dark that she could not even see the trees outlined against the sky. It was no wonder. There were no trees at all. No bushes. No shade or shelter anywhere. Just mats of tiny plants that clung to the baked earth here and there, making a patchwork of pink, gold, and dull green.

Between the plant mats there was smooth, bone-dry clay scattered with lumpy, mottled rocks. The plain shimmered with waves of heat that rose from its dried-up surface like hot breath. And something flashed on the horizon, a blinding glare, as though another sun burned there.

Rowan looked up, squinting. Not the tiniest speck marred the clear, hot blue of the sky. There were no fearsome creatures circling for prey. Just a ball of white heat beating down on the shrinking land, heating it as flame heats an oven.

> *But dangers seek you as you go,*
> *One from above . . .*

He felt a hand on his shoulder. Allun was standing beside him, staring at him gravely.

Rowan swallowed. "The danger of the rhyme—

the danger that threatens by day and hides by night. It is the sun," he said.

Allun nodded briefly. "So it seems. This is why we did not wake you. We realized as soon as we saw this accursed plain that we could not cross it by day. The delay is unfortunate, but our only chance of surviving is to travel by night. If we begin at sunset and do not spare ourselves we may reach the city before the sun rises again."

"The danger of the night—" Rowan began.

"Whatever danger the darkness holds for us," Allun interrupted, "it can be no worse than being baked alive." He pressed his lips together. "As would be happening at this moment, in the midst of the plain, if I had had my way. Perlain would be dried and dead, and we would be about to join him. When will I learn sense?"

He turned and stumbled back down the sand dunes. Rowan followed, shaken by the bitterness of his words. Allun pretended so well to be an uncaring joker that sometimes it was hard to remember that he was not nearly as confident as he seemed.

While they had been gone, Perlain and Zeel had made a tent, using long sticks, the wet blanket, and Zeel's kite. They were sitting huddled underneath it, sheltering from the sun and talking in low voices.

Allun and Rowan crawled under the shelter with them. Perlain took his knife from his belt and carefully cut four small, equal slices from the hard brown seaweed cake. He gave one slice to each of them and took the last for himself.

Rowan chewed the tough food gratefully. It seemed a long time since he had eaten, and though the cake's seaweed taste was very strong, he did not find it too unpleasing. Zeel sniffed her portion suspiciously, then began to nibble at it without appetite. Allun looked at his with pretended disdain.

"As a baker of some renown, I must protest that you call this 'cake,' Perlain," he said. "If we are to live on this, we will have turned into very thin fish before a week is out."

"Better to be a live thin fish than dead of hunger," Perlain remarked, unconcerned. "But as you wish." He finished his own cake with relish, licked the last crumbs from his fingers, then took a drink from the water bag.

"A little water to follow," he said. "But a little only. Supplies are short."

Allun nodded gloomily and began to eat, wrinkling his nose as he did so. Perlain smiled slightly and crawled out from under the shelter.

"While you are resting here, I will soak," he

announced, peering back in at them. "Then I will be ready when the sun begins to set. Sleep well."

Rowan waited until Zeel and Allun had settled themselves to rest, then crept out of the tent. He found the Maris man standing at the edge of the water, looking out at the glittering sea.

"Perlain, you cannot come with us into the Wastelands," he said abruptly. "What if we are still traveling when morning comes? There is no shade. There will be little water to drink or to wet your skin. You will die, Perlain."

"I am in danger whether I go or stay," answered Perlain. "There is no fresh water on the shore, and if I try to escape by swimming, the night and the serpents will come before I reach land. I have considered this well, and I have decided that if I am to die, I prefer to do it with my friends than to do it alone. A fish-man out of water I began, and so I will end."

Rowan tried to speak, but his throat was tight and he could not.

Perlain's thin lips curved in a smile. "I do not regret that I joined you, Rowan," he murmured. "Without me you would certainly have perished in the sea long before we were in sight of land. So I have played my part. As Allun and Zeel, and you yourself, will no doubt play yours, before the quest is done."

He walked into the water and lay down in the shallows. "But I will not die before my time," he said, closing his eyes. "Now go and rest, Rowan. You must gather all your strength. For who knows what the evening will bring?"

10 ⚭ THE DANGER OF THE NIGHT

They set off just before sunset, when the sun was scarlet fire burning low on the horizon ahead. The sky was stained red. Even the air seemed red as they left the sand of the dunes and began to move across the expanse of flat rocks, still hot underfoot.

They walked quickly, heads bowed so that the sun would not burn their eyes, watching their feet so they would not stumble.

"The rhyme said our way would be hard and stony," complained Allun. "But it did not warn us of cooked feet. These rocks are like baking trays just out of the oven."

"They will cool soon enough," said Zeel. "Later it will be cold, I think. It is always so in large, empty spaces such as this."

"I am pleased to hear it," Perlain called back over his shoulder. He was well ahead, almost running over the stones, eager to reach the softer, cooler ground beyond. He wore the dampened blanket around his head and shoulders to protect him from the last of the drying heat.

"Perhaps if the sun above is the danger by day, cold is the danger that will threaten us from below, in the night," Allun suggested.

"We can deal with cold," said Zeel crisply. "We will huddle together and wrap ourselves in the silk of the kite for warmth. Tor, Mithren, and I have done this often—in the past."

Her voice changed as she said the last words. Her usually strong, eager face was downcast. It looked softened and lost.

She misses her people, Rowan thought. She wonders if she will ever again fly with Tor and Mithren over the green fields or walk with Ogden, barefoot upon the grass. She wonders if she will ever again see her home.

He saw Zeel look up, frowning, into the blazing distance where still the flashes of silver that marked the Zebak city mingled with the scarlet of the sky.

That city was once her home. The thought came to him suddenly, with a small shock. How easy it was to forget that Zeel was not a Traveler born, but a Zebak. Did she remember anything of her past life? Were any memories, good or bad, stirring within her at this moment?

"At last! We are coming to the end of these accursed rocks!" Allun's exclamation broke into Rowan's thoughts, and Rowan turned his eyes to the way ahead.

Sure enough, the tightly packed rocks were at last giving way to the smooth, cracked clay and the plant mats that they had seen from the sand dunes. There were mottled, lumpy stones scattered about as well, certainly, but these could be avoided with ease.

Perlain had already reached the edge of the rocks. He glanced behind him, smiling at his companions with relief, and stepped onto the clay.

And then, with a cry of shock, he threw up his hands and disappeared from sight.

"Perlain!" shrieked Rowan. But he could hardly hear his own voice—or the voices of Allun and Zeel. For as they shouted, it was as if the whole plain cried out with them and began to move.

The mottled lumps were alive. They were heaving themselves up, spreading scaly wings, leaving the flat rocks on which they had squatted and scrambling into the air. Like a vast flock of hideous, swollen, featherless birds, the creatures fought for space, hissing and screeching in their fright. And from beneath the earth there came another sound—an evil scratching, clicking sound that chilled the blood.

Zeel had reached the edge of the rocks and was already scrambling down into the hole in the earth where Perlain had disappeared.

"Perlain, here!" she cried, stretching out her hand. And then the scratching sound came again, louder this time, and her voice rose to a shrill scream. "Oh, by my life! Allun! Help me!"

The flying, swooping creatures filled the air in their thousands, hiding the edge of the rocks from Rowan's sight. Desperately he pushed forward, holding up his arms to protect his eyes. The scaly things dashed against his back, head, and shoulders, clinging to his clothes and hair with their small claws, flapping their wings frantically. Shuddering, he plucked at them, trying to tear them off.

"Rowan!" he heard Allun calling. "Here! Here!" And Zeel was screaming, "Oh, I cannot hold him. It has him! Oh, help me!"

Rowan turned and ran blindly toward the sound.

And finally he was at the edge of the rocks, where Allun was stretched out facedown, his arms around Zeel's waist, pulling, pulling with all his strength.

Zeel was lying half in and half out of a shallow hole with her arms stretched out toward a yawning pit of blackness at one side. In an instant, Rowan understood. Perlain had fallen into a tunnel that ran beneath the plain. The thin layer of clay that had formed the tunnel's roof had collapsed under his weight.

At first Rowan could not see Perlain at all. Then he realized that Zeel's thin brown hands were clutching Perlain's ankles. The rest of his body was hidden in the darkness of the tunnel. Zeel was trying to pull Perlain back, but something was pulling against her with enormous strength.

"I cannot hold him!" she cried again.

"Rowan, help me!" shouted Allun.

Rowan stood, frozen. A dozen thoughts were clamoring in his terrified mind. He could take hold of Allun and help him pull. He could leap down into the hole with Zeel and try to help her free Perlain from whatever had attacked him.

But he knew he was not strong enough for his efforts to make more than a tiny difference. His fear might give him strength for one great effort, but the strength would not last. Not for long enough.

With a sudden jerk Zeel was pulled forward, and Allun with her.

"Rowan!" Allun shouted. He fought to keep his

grip, desperately trying to drag Zeel back toward the rocks.

The ground beyond the hole shifted as whatever was beneath the earth, whatever had seen Perlain as its prey, thrashed in fury. Clay cracked and crumbled in a long, crooked line, showing clearly the path of the tunnel that ran just below its surface and the long, twisting shape of the beast within it.

There was a low and terrible growling sound. The clay cracked further. The mottled creatures shrieked and scattered in terror, their wings buffeting Rowan's face, forcing him to duck his head so that he stared at the stones beneath his feet.

The stones . . .

"Rowan!"

One great effort . . .

Barely thinking what he was doing, Rowan bent and wrestled a great stone from the ground. Muscles straining, he lifted the stone above his head and pitched it with all his strength down onto the line of cracking clay.

"Now!" he yelled at the same moment. "Allun! Zeel! Pull now!"

The stone smashed through the clay and thudded onto whatever was underneath.

There was a rasping cry, the earth heaved, and suddenly Allun was staggering backward, pulling

Zeel back onto the rocks, and Perlain's limp body was coming with her, sliding out of the earth like a cork pulled from a bottle.

"Get him back!" shrieked Rowan, rushing to help as they lifted the Maris man onto the stones. "Back!"

But they had only managed to take a few paces when the rock Rowan had thrown was heaved to one side in a shower of clay and the growling beast beneath the earth was twisting forward in pursuit of them.

It burst through the hole in its ruined tunnel, rearing up, lunging at them, its huge, curved pincers opening and closing, tearing at the air, the shining red-brown segments of its huge body rippling as it moved, its thousand tiny legs wriggling like horned worms.

Zeel screamed—a high-pitched, terrified scream that was even more horrible to Rowan than the beast's own growling cry.

Holding Perlain between them, they turned and ran for their lives, stumbling back over the stones, expecting every moment to hear the sound of the beast at their heels.

But there was no sound. And when finally they looked behind them, there was nothing to be seen but the red sky and the plain and the small, lumpy flying creatures circling uncertainly above it.

With a sobbing cry Zeel collapsed onto the rocks with her head in her hands. Allun and Rowan lowered Perlain gently till he lay beside her. The Maris man was covered in clay from head to foot. His eyes seemed sealed shut.

Allun knelt and pressed his ear to Perlain's chest. Rowan watched, holding his breath, giving a long sigh of relief when Allun raised his head and nodded.

He took the water bag and moistened Perlain's lips. "You are safe, Perlain," he whispered. "The blanket must have protected you from harm. And the creature has gone. Perlain, wake."

At last Perlain's eyes opened. They were glazed with fear.

"Serpent!" he hissed.

"No." Beside him, Zeel was shuddering. "Ishkin."

Allun and Rowan looked at her in astonishment. Her face was white under the film of clay, and her mouth was trembling. Never had Rowan expected to see strong Zeel look like this.

"Zeel, you remember," he said, suddenly understanding.

She moistened her lips, and nodded. "I . . . remember a picture," she said huskily. "A picture . . . horrible, frightening. They used to show it to me, when I was bad. When I . . . disobeyed. I had forgotten it. Till just then, when I saw—"

She broke off, then forced herself to go on. "There were words, too. They would all point at me, and they would chant a rhyme. I remember it. I remember being so afraid. It went:

> *"Bad child, wicked child, push you in the bin,*
> *Out with the rubbish on your chin, chin, chin.*
> *Up pops an ishkin, then it pulls you in,*
> *Makes you cry and sucks you dry and throws*
> *away the skin."*

Her voice trailed off. She was shaking all over.

Rowan felt his own skin crawling. What sort of people would terrify a tiny child like this? Zeel had been only two, at the most, when she was found by the Travelers.

Zeel pressed her hands together to stop them from shaking, and tried to laugh. "Just a children's rhyme," she muttered. "It is foolish of me to fear it now." But still she shuddered as though she would never stop.

Rowan and Allun exchanged glances. "Not so foolish, my friend," said Allun lightly. "Now I have seen this ishkin for myself, the idea of meeting it again is not at all to my liking."

"There is not just one," said Zeel. She closed her eyes. "There are many. Many, many. The ground is full of them."

Leaving Perlain and Zeel to rest, Allun and Rowan walked back to the edge of the rocks. The sun had dipped below the horizon and the moon had risen. The plain was still. The mottled flying creatures were clustered on the flat rocks once more.

"The ishkin, it seems, do not normally attack on the surface," Allun said. "They wait for prey to fall through the clay. The lumpy flying lizard things are safe upon the rocks."

"I cannot understand why there are so many flying lizards." Rowan scanned the strange scene before him. "I have seen no insects or small creatures that could be their prey. And they do not graze upon the plants. How do they feed?"

As he spoke, there was a quarrel among one group of the creatures, and two were pushed aside. One flapped clumsily into the air. The other, less fortunate, fell, scrabbling, onto the clay.

Instantly, the ground collapsed beneath its body. There was a rushing, scratching sound, and the creature was dragged, shrieking, into darkness. Its companions chattered for a moment, then went back to their rest.

Rowan turned his head away, sickened.

"We know how the ishkin feed, in any case," said Allun grimly. "No doubt the whole plain is undermined by their tunnels. Look there."

He pointed to the place where only half an hour earlier they had struggled so desperately to save Perlain. Already the tunnel had been repaired. The earth that formed its roof was as smooth as it had ever been.

"Sheba's rhyme said, 'Hard and stony is your way.'" Rowan looked again out at the plain—at the treacherously smooth clay, at the mats of small prickly plants, and finally at the flat stones where the flying creatures clustered. "Perhaps the stones . . ."

Allun nodded. "Yes," he said. "If the stones are the only places where the lumpy lizards are safe, it seems that we will have to be lumpies ourselves. Lumpies without wings. We will have to leap from one stone to the next to cross these accursed Wastelands."

He took a deep breath. "Very well, Rowan. What must be, must be. We will rouse Perlain and Zeel and begin at once. If we are to reach the city by sunrise, there is no time to lose."

11 ⤳ AGAINST THE WALL

Rowan was silent. The thought of the perilous journey ahead filled him with dread.

If anyone should fail to make a jump successfully, he or she would stumble onto the treacherous clay. Then, in the blink of an eye, the unlucky one would be caught and dragged away by one of the beasts that waited below.

Words from the children's rhyme that Zeel had repeated went around and around in his head. Foolish, horrible words.

> *Up pops an ishkin, then it pulls you in,*
> *Makes you cry and sucks you dry and throws*
> *away the skin.*

His stomach churned when he remembered the shriek of the flying creature as it was dragged under the earth, remembered the sight of the ishkin as it reared up, its great curved pincers snapping, its tiny hooked legs clawing.

Yet he knew Allun was right. They had to cross the plain somehow, and there was no other way.

"Perlain is weak with shock," he managed to say at last. "And Zeel . . . is afraid."

Allun swung round to face him. "And you and I are not afraid, I suppose?" he demanded fiercely.

Rowan stared, unable to find an answer. Allun returned his gaze. "Fear will make us stumble, Rowan," he said, more gently. "So we must pretend confidence even if we do not feel it. We must pretend so well that we begin to believe."

His lean face broke into its familiar clown's grin, and he clapped Rowan on the shoulder. "I, for one, am used to pretending. I have done it all my life. Playing the fool to hide my real feelings is my one great talent. Now is my chance to use it."

For many hours, in single file, they leaped from one stone to the next, zigzagging across the plain as the moon shone cold above them. Allun led the way, moving quickly, taking the easiest path, but one that led as directly as possible toward the small glow on the horizon.

The plain seemed to boil with movement as all

around them the ishkin took their prey. The mottled flying creatures that Allun called "lumpies" were
many, and fought together often, so that time and
again the horrible scene that he and Rowan had
witnessed was repeated.

But never did Allun look down or aside. He
looked only forward. His pockets were filled with
pebbles, and these he threw to startle the creatures
clustered on the stone ahead. "Move aside, lumpies," he would shout. "Make room!"

The lumpies would flap into the air, shrieking
and hissing crossly. Allun would leap at once, while
the stone was clear. Then he would choose his next
landing place, toss another pebble, and leap again.

All the time he called back to Perlain, Zeel, and
Rowan, who were following him. His voice
drowned the scratching, rushing sounds of the
ishkin attacks, the despairing shrieks of the victims.
He was never silent, never still. He encouraged,
joked, whistled, even sang.

"I have always fancied myself as a dancer," he
would call. "What an excellent way this is to practice my art." And the next time he leaped, he would
spread his arms wide, making himself look ridicu-
lous as possible. Then he would make up a rhyme
about a frog or a jumping insect and leap on, croak-
ing or chirruping to make them smile.

He asked them riddles, made fun of wise sayings, invented insulting stories about everyone they knew. His voice grew hoarse with shouting.

When he stopped for a few minutes to rest, he sang long, loud songs and insisted they join in. If they failed to answer him, he teased them. He would taunt Perlain about his flat feet, call Rowan "skinny rabbit," or wonder aloud at the uselessness of Zeel's fine yellow kite when there was no wind to drive it.

It was foolish. It was annoying. But Rowan knew that it was saving their lives. It was taking their minds from their fear, forcing them to look ahead, and drowning the terrifying sounds of the plain. It was helping them to leap cleanly, saving them from the faltering clumsiness that would come if they remembered the fate that awaited them should they fall.

So he did his best to shout back at Allun's insults, groan at his jokes, and join his singing, though his legs were trembling with weariness and with every jump he felt that he could jump no more. Zeel and Perlain, beating back their own suffering, did the same.

And so, hour after painful hour, as the moon sank lower in the sky and the glow on the horizon grew larger and brighter, they went on.

In the darkness just before dawn, Rowan realized that the way had suddenly become easier. The flat stones were more numerous, dotting the clay every-where, even touching one another in places. It was no longer necessary to jump. He could step from one stone to the next in safety.

The lumpies had become more numerous, too. They were flocking so thickly that they had become a nuisance. They filled the air, crowded every stone, and quarreled loudly as they jostled for space. More and more arrived every moment.

Are they following us? Rowan thought, puzzled. They certainly seem to be. And yet they did not follow us before. Can it be because we are nearing the city?

He looked ahead at the glow, which he had at last realized was flame gushing from the top of a tall tower or chimney that rose high above the city. Other, smaller, lights were now visible, too. They were few, but they stretched away on both sides of the tower as far as he could see, shining above a layer of darkness that he guessed was a high wall. The city was huge and seemed to be totally encircled.

He had been concentrating so hard on reaching the city that he had given no real thought to what they were to do when they arrived. But now that the goal was so near and he could see its vastness, questions began rushing into his mind.

How were they going to find Annad in a place so

large, let alone free her? How were they going to
remain hidden while they searched?

"We should stop for a moment and talk, I think,"
called Allun quietly. For some time now his voice
had been lower. They were very near the city.
There could be patrols on the watch, though it was
hard to believe that the Zebak could expect invasion from the direction of this desolate plain. It was
truly the city's "back door."

Weary but relieved, they crouched in a circle,
each safely upon a rock. They passed around the
food and the water bags, and each of them drank
deeply. They felt they could afford to do so, now
that the Wastelands had been safely crossed.

Lumpies squabbled and flapped around them.

"Why are they gathering here?" whispered Zeel,
batting them away from her impatiently. "They are
coming from all over the plain, as if on purpose to
annoy us."

"They are useful to us, in fact," Allun said. "No
one could see us in this crowd, even if they looked
over the wall. Or hear us, either."

Perlain was gazing up at the sky, wetting his face and
hands with water. Rowan glanced at him, worried. The
Maris man seemed very ill. He needed to soak. He
needed rest. And sunrise was not far away. Soon that
glaring ball would climb above the horizon at their

backs, heating the earth and the air—hotter, hotter . . .

"What is our plan? Are we to climb the wall? Or walk along it to try to find a gate?" Rowan asked.

"A gate may be hours away, and we do not know which direction to try. Also, gates mean guards. It will be far safer and quicker to climb," said Zeel firmly.

Allun shook his head. "It will not be safer or quicker for Perlain—or for Rowan."

"Or for you, Allun the baker, I have no doubt," said Zeel, grinning, taking her revenge for the way Allun had teased her during the long night. "But you have done your part. You brought us through the Wastelands with your clowning. Now it is my turn to—what did you say?—'practice my art.' I will climb the wall, find a place to fasten the rope, and pull you up after me, one by one. But it must be done in darkness."

They hurried forward, almost running in their haste, but soon they had to slow again. They had left the clay behind completely and reached the solid rock on which the city was built. There they found themselves wading through a thick layer of sticks and stones that threatened to trip them at every step. The lumpies, too, were so many that it was almost impossible to walk between them or to see the way ahead.

There are thousands of them, thought Rowan, stopping for a moment. They could overwhelm us if they chose.

He shivered nervously. Yet surely there was no reason to fear the creatures. Despite their ugly appearance, the spines on their backs and their sharp little claws and teeth, they had not seemed dangerous—except, occasionally, to one another.

Suddenly he realized that he had lost sight of Allun, Zeel, and Perlain. "Allun!" he whispered urgently. "I cannot see you. Where are you?"

"Here. Straight ahead of you. We have reached the wall, Rowan." But instead of sounding triumphant, Allun's voice was strained and odd. Rowan headed blindly toward the sound and almost bumped into Perlain, who was standing motionless while lumpies swarmed around him.

"What is it?" Rowan hissed.

Perlain pointed.

Allun and Zeel were together just ahead of them, facing the wall. Allun was staring at it in despair. Zeel was running her hands over its surface as though she had to touch it to believe the evidence of her own eyes.

For the wall was not made of brick, stone, or wood, full of joins and toeholds that could be used by a climber. It was made of metal—polished sheet metal that rose smooth and slippery to a sharp edge high above their heads.

Rowan stared at it, dumbfounded, realizing several things at once.

He realized that here was the source of the distant flash he had seen when first he looked over the plain. It had been the glinting of this metal as it was caught by the newly risen sun.

He realized that though the metal was cold now, by midmorning it would be too hot to touch. It would radiate heat over the plain and everything in it. To stand beside it as he was doing now would be like standing in a fire.

He realized that no one could climb this wall unaided and that the sharp edge at the top would slice Zeel's rope through in a moment.

Could we tunnel under the wall instead? he thought wildly. He crouched and scrabbled at the ground. And then he cried out as he realized the last and most horrifying thing of all.

He and his friends were not the first to have stood, despairing, in this place.

For the pale-colored sticks and stones through which he had been wading so awkwardly for the last few minutes were not sticks and stones at all.

They were bleached white bones.

12 ∞ THE MIRROR CRACKS

"How many poor wretches have been thrown into the Wastelands to die?" muttered Allun. "How many thousands, over the centuries, to create this—this horror."

He stared with loathing at the lumpies, whose reason for massing in such numbers, and at this place, now seemed horribly clear.

"Look at them—waiting for us to die in our turn, so they can pick our bones," he growled. "You asked how they fed, Rowan. Now you have your answer."

"It may not be," Rowan said in a low voice. But the lumpies were crowding in, pressing them to the wall, hissing in their eagerness. They were so close that he could see their forked tongues flicking in and out and their small, hungry eyes.

Now he could see how much they resembled the

creature that had snatched Annad. They were its smaller relations, and what they lacked in size and strength they made up in numbers.

"Get away!" Zeel stepped forward threateningly, and the lumpies scattered. But only for a moment. Soon they were creeping back, pressing in once more.

The four companions stood staring at the wall.

At their backs the sky was lightening, turning pink. The wall had begun to reflect the color. It had also begun dimly to reflect their tired, pale faces, and the lumpies crowding around them like creatures from a nightmare.

On both sides the wall stretched into the distance—endless shining metal plates, fused together. There was no hole or gap. No knob or catch. No sign of a gate. No possibility of escape from the heat to come. And bones glimmered on the ground as far as the eye could see.

"Have we come so far, and suffered so much, only to die within sight of this accursed city?" cried Allun.

Suddenly Sheba's words came into Rowan's mind. *When you really need them . . .*

He pulled the oilcloth package from his shirt and took out one of the four remaining sticks. "Zeel, we must start a fire," he said urgently. "We must see if Sheba can help us."

Zeel pressed her lips together. "The witch lured us to this place of death with her instruction to follow the light. She has betrayed us."

"It is true." Allun's face was grim. "For her own reasons, or for pure wickedness, Sheba wishes us never to return to Rin."

Rowan could not believe it. He *would* not. He glanced at Perlain. The Maris man was leaning against the wall. His eyes were closed.

"Zeel, please! The flint!" he begged. "Give it to me. I must try. The sun is about to rise. The heat will soon begin. And Perlain . . ." He broke off, unable to finish.

He threw himself to his knees and scrabbled among the bones, collecting dead leaves and twigs blown from the desert plants. When he had enough to make a tiny blaze, he heaped them up in front of him, with the stick balanced on top. Then he held out his hand.

Grudgingly, Zeel gave him the flint. Rowan struck a spark, and the dry leaves and twigs on their bed of bones caught immediately, first smoking and then bursting into flames.

The stick flickered green, then flared up strongly. Sheba's face appeared, wavering, in the blaze. Rowan stared, caught and held by the image—by its growing strength, its deep red eyes. His right hand began to burn so that he almost cried out in pain. And then the voice came to him:

> At dawn the enemy attacks,
> As hunger howls, the mirror cracks.
> Then, pressed against that shining wall,
> Like worms among the bones you'll crawl.
> It's useless now to fight or plead—
> Squirm softly, while the creatures feed.

Horrified, Rowan jumped up and kicked at the fire, stamping it out, crushing the ashes to powder. The throbbing pain in his hand slowly died, but Sheba's terrible words still burned in his mind.

"What did she say?" asked Perlain faintly. He was still leaning against the wall. His face looked shriveled and white.

The terrible tiredness that had gripped Rowan when he burned the first of Sheba's sticks was sweeping over him again. He could not bring himself to repeat the rhyme, but he knew he had to tell the truth.

"She jeered at us," he mumbled. "Zeel was right. Sheba led us here to die."

Perlain closed his eyes. "So be it," he said calmly.

"Do not say that, Perlain!" Zeel's eyes snapped with fury. "Are we to wait tamely to bake?"

"The sun is rising," warned Allun.

At dawn the enemy attacks . . .

The wall flashed blindingly, catching the sun's first rays. The lumpies surged forward, crying out hungrily.

As hunger howls . . .

And then there was another sound. It came from the wall. Rowan spun to face it. His eyes watering in the glare, he saw his own reflection. He saw the reflections of his friends and the lumpies flocking, fighting one another for space. And he saw something else—something that at first he could not believe.

A crack was appearing in the wall, right beside Perlain. The crack ran down one of the seams from the top to the bottom. It was as though the seam was splitting.

. . . the mirror cracks . . .

Rowan shouted, pointing. His voice was drowned by the lumpies' screeching, but Zeel and Allun had already seen what was happening. They stood openmouthed.

The crack grew wider, wider. One whole section of the wall was swinging outward, like a door. It was being pushed open from the other side. Something was coming through. Something big, making a heavy, rumbling sound.

Then, pressed against that shining wall,
Like worms among the bones you'll crawl. . . .

"Quickly! Move hard against the wall! Hide!" Rowan shouted, struggling to Perlain's side. He dragged the almost unconscious Maris man to the ground.

Zeel and Allun lunged forward, throwing themselves down beside the wall with Rowan and Perlain, burying themselves as deeply as possible in the bleached white bones.

Just in time. For the next moment the wall was fully open and a huge covered cart was lumbering through. Four Zebak were pushing the cart, grunting with the effort.

"What sort of job is this for trained guards?" the man nearest to Rowan growled. "One urk with a grach could do it."

His heavy boots crunched on the bones beside Rowan's head. As he passed, Rowan peered up at him cautiously. He was very tall and broad shouldered in his steel gray uniform. His pale eyes were angry. The black streak that ran down his forehead from hair to nose made him look cruel and stern.

"The grach have more important duties," snapped the guard next to him. "You have your orders, Zanel. Do not question them, or you will find yourself locked out in the Wastelands, as many have been before you!"

"Choosing between the ishkin and the wall," added another of the guards, snickering.

Zanel kicked angrily at the lumpies flocking around his feet, but he said nothing more.

Rowan lay motionless beside Perlain, his heart pounding. The guards had passed. The door into the city was wide open. But he did not dare move. The guards had not noticed them yet, but one of them could turn and do so at any moment. And then there would be no escape and no mercy.

It's useless now to fight or plead—

The guards began to work two levers, one on each side of the cart. With a grinding sound, the back of the cart began to tip. At the same time the cover wound back.

A stinking flood of vegetable and meat scraps began pouring onto the ground. The lumpies screeched with one voice and fell on the food. In their thousands they fought and flapped around the cart and the guards in a hideous confusion of scaly wings, mottled bodies, and grasping claws. The guards, scraping out the last of the rubbish, yelled and beat at them angrily. The creatures' noise was deafening.

Squirm softly, while the creatures feed.

The moment had come. Rowan wriggled forward, dragging Perlain with him, keeping his head down. He felt Allun and Zeel helping from behind as he crawled through the gap in the wall and into the city beyond.

They lay in the shadow of the wall, panting with fear, looking quickly around them. They were in a large square paved with red bricks. The square was littered with scraps of food that had fallen from the cart and was deserted. It was too early for anyone but the guards on duty to be awake, it seemed.

A narrow road ahead led to a tall building topped by the flaming chimney they had seen from the plain. Other lower, longer buildings squatted on either side of the square, their doors firmly closed. The place smelled sourly of smoke and garbage.

Where should they go? Where could they hide? Soon the guards would be trundling the empty cart back into the square. There was no time to lose.

Bells began to ring somewhere in the center of the city. They clanged on and on. Waking the sleeping people. Stirring the city into life.

"Water . . ." groaned Perlain. He waved his hand to their left.

Zeel tugged at Rowan's arm. He saw that she was also looking to the left. To a place beside one of the buildings, where a flight of metal steps led down into the ground.

Rowan hesitated, but not for long. The cart was coming back. Already he could see its front wheels rolling through the gap in the wall.

He nodded, and together he, Zeel, and Allun, with Perlain held between them, ran for the steps. The mingled sounds of cart wheels on bricks and the screeching of the feeding lumpies floated after them as they hurried down, down into darkness.

At the bottom of the steps was a door. Allun turned the handle carefully. The door opened and they slipped inside.

They found themselves in a brightly lit passage. It was lined with metal, like the metal of the wall. There was a distant thumping, roaring sound.

"There is a creature here," whispered Zeel, putting her hand to the knife at her belt.

Rowan shook his head, puzzled. "It does not sound like an animal. It is—regular. Like millstones grinding."

"A machine, then," whispered Allun. "Do not worry about it. We must find Perlain some water, and quickly. If he does not soak soon he will die."

His forehead was creased in a worried frown as he glanced at Perlain's closed eyes and pale face.

They went on along the corridor. It was eerie to

see their own reflections moving along with them on both sides.

"It is like walking in a crowd," said Allun. "A foolish crowd of oddities in a corridor under an enemy city, without an idea of where they are going."

They reached a point where the corridor branched into two, and stopped, wondering whether to go left or right.

"There," a voice croaked.

It was Perlain who had spoken. He pointed feebly to the right.

They took the righthand passage, hurrying as fast as they dared. The sound of the machinery grew louder.

The corridor branched again and again. Many other smaller passages ran from each main way. All were deserted. All were brightly lit and lined with the same shining metal. None had any doors that they could see. But each time there was a choice to make, Perlain pointed and they obeyed.

13 ∾ THE MAZE

At first Rowan tried to keep their path fixed in his mind, but he soon gave up. There were too many turns, and every passage looked the same. As well, now that the immediate danger of discovery by the guards had passed, the terrible tiredness he had felt by the wall was sweeping over him again. It was an effort to put one foot after the other. All he wanted to do was lie down and sleep.

"This is folly," muttered Allun as they turned for the tenth or twelfth time. "We will never find our way out of this maze."

Rowan could hardly hear him. The thumping, roaring noise was very loud now, and he was almost asleep on his feet.

"If this is a maze, I think we have reached the center," he heard Zeel say.

He looked up wearily and saw what Zeel meant. At the end of the passage they had just entered was a shining metal door. A small black-and-white picture was fixed to it, but he could not see what it was.

With every step they took, the roaring noise became louder. But still Rowan could hear Perlain gasping painfully as he struggled on between Allun and Zeel, trying to hurry.

At last they were close enough to see the picture on the door clearly. It was a grinning white skull in a black square.

They halted abruptly.

"This does not look promising." Allun frowned.

"It does not mean that there is danger for all inside the door. It means that the place is forbidden, and the penalty for entering is death," Zeel said slowly.

She saw them looking at her in surprise, and shrugged. "I remember," she said. "It must be one of the first things we are taught."

We, thought Rowan through his haze of tiredness. This is the first time I have heard Zeel say "we" when talking of the Zebak. He glanced at her troubled face and an uncomfortable feeling stirred in his chest.

Perlain struggled weakly, trying to make Zeel and Allun move on. They supported him as he staggered to the door. It was fastened with a padlock. He plucked helplessly at the lock with his webbed hands and moaned.

"Perlain, how could there be water in there?" Allun asked gently.

"There is . . . water," croaked Perlain, clawing at the door. "I . . . must . . ."

Zeel, her face stern and set, pulled her knife from her belt. Rowan felt a pang of fear. But then she knelt, took the padlock in her sun-browned hands, and began working away at it with the sharp point. "This I learned from the Travelers," she muttered. "The Travelers do not care for locks. Or penalties."

After a few agonizing minutes the padlock clicked and came loose. Zeel stood back, biting her lip. Rowan realized immediately that, though she had broken the lock, she could not make herself push the door open.

He stepped forward to do it for her, but Perlain was there before him. The door swung open, and an almost deafening roar came from the dark, echoing space beyond. Perlain took no notice. Before anyone could stop him, he had plunged through the doorway.

Rowan and Allun started after him. Zeel followed reluctantly. Plainly, she was afraid. Rowan wondered again at the strength of her early training. Like her fear of the ishkin, her fear of the sign was something she could not control.

Light from the corridor streamed into the room beyond the door, shining on a metal floor. But as soon as they were inside, Zeel pushed the door shut and stood against it.

Then the blackness was complete. The space pulsed with sound—roaring, rushing sound. Rowan could see nothing. He reached out blindly. "Allun! Perlain!" he shouted in panic.

"I am here," called Perlain's voice. "But do not move. It is not safe for you."

There was a clatter from somewhere to Rowan's right, and Allun bellowed in pain.

Rowan began to edge toward the sound, his heart beating wildly.

"It is all right. I hit my head on something, clumsy fool that I am!" Allun shouted. "What was it? Wait! I think . . . yes!" There was a scratching noise, and a small light appeared. It glowed, then brightened. At last Rowan could see Allun's face, smeared with a streak of sooty oil, and his hand holding up a grimy oil lamp.

Allun grinned. "If it was necessary to hit something, I am glad it was this," he said. "It was hanging just beside me, here, with striking matches on a shelf beside it, all complete. Now we shall see where we are."

He held the lamp high and moved it slowly around. Rowan gasped.

They were standing on a metal platform that hung over the edge of a vast underground lake—a lake as large as the bukshah field in Rin. Beside them, taking up most of the platform's space, squatted a monstrous machine that chugged and throbbed unceasingly. The lamp had hung from a shelf at its side. On the shelf were some gloves, a few tools, and a can of oil.

Allun pointed at the silver pipes that snaked up from the water, climbed the walls, and disappeared into holes in the roof.

"They pump water up to the city from here," he exclaimed in amazement. "The lake is like a huge well. This machine must be a great pump that works by itself. Who could believe such a thing?"

Rowan glanced at the door. Zeel was standing there, utterly still and silent. Her face was pale and tense.

He turned back to Allun, and together they crept cautiously to the edge of the platform, knelt, and peered over the edge. In the black water below them floated Perlain. His eyes were closed, but they

could see that he had come to no harm. He was
regaining his strength, slowly but surely. Already he
was not so pale, and he was breathing steadily.

Looking down, Allun shuddered. Rowan knew
what he was thinking. If they had stumbled over the
edge of the platform in the dark and fallen into that
dark, deep water, they would certainly have
drowned. Perlain would have been too weak to save
them.

As if he felt their gaze, Perlain's eyes opened. He
looked up at them and smiled peacefully.

"You were right, Perlain," Allun called to him.

"Of course. A Maris can smell water wherever it
lies," Perlain answered drowsily.

"Rest and soak, Perlain," Rowan called. "We will
be back soon."

"One hour," said Perlain, and his eyes closed once
more. Rowan's own eyelids drooped as he watched.
He was so tired. So tired . . .

He shook himself. There was no time for sleep.
He turned away from the lake and followed Allun
and his light to the door where Zeel still waited.

"This place is probably as safe as any for us to
rest," Allun said above the roaring of the pump. "A
little noisy, perhaps, but one cannot ask for everything."

Wordlessly, Zeel held out her hand for the lamp.

Allun looked surprised but gave it to her. She looked at it carefully, turning it around and around, careless of the black grease it left on her fingers.

She remembers lamps like this, guessed Rowan, watching her fascinated eyes. She was probably warned not to touch them. Yet she was attracted by the flame, as young children are. So she remembers.

Zeel put the lamp on the floor and looked up at Rowan. "Before we rest, you must burn another of the witch's sticks," she said abruptly. "I must know what is to befall us."

Rowan hesitated. His hand throbbed as if it already felt the pain that would come when another stick was burned. And he had only three sticks left. Was their need great enough for him to use one now? He turned uncertainly to Allun.

Allun nodded. "If Sheba has advice to give, we should have it. Then we will be prepared should the owners of this lamp pay us a visit in the next hour."

Reluctantly, Rowan brought out the package from his shirt, unwrapped the oilcloth, and took out a stick. Before doing anything else, he carefully rewrapped the last two sticks and put them away. As he did, he felt the medallion, warm against his hand. What part does it play in all this? he asked himself. Is it the medallion that helps me hear Sheba's words, perhaps?

"Burn the stick, Rowan!" cried Zeel impatiently. "Why do you wait? Thrust it into the lamp's flame."

Before he could think about it further, Rowan did as she asked. Green fire ran up and down the stick's length, flickering higher, higher, till shadows leaped on all their faces and on the door behind them.

This time the pain in Rowan's hand was so great and came so suddenly that tears sprang into his eyes. Blinking through a watery haze, he saw Sheba's face appear in the flame. It seemed to grin at him, its red eyes blazing. And then came the words:

> *The one who first heard Zebak bells*
> *Must use the truth the mirror tells.*
> *The hand must bleed to reach the end,*
> *One finger stands, the others bend.*
> *With chains and sorrow you must pay*
> *For other hands to guide your way.*

The green fire wavered and died. The ashes of the stick fell to the ground. The oil lamp flickered and went out, as though its strength had been completely consumed. They were in darkness again.

Trying to keep his voice steady, Rowan repeated the rhyme. He could not see the others, but he had no doubt that their faces were dismayed.

The rhyme did not help. It did not tell them what

to do if they were caught in this place. It did not tell them how to get out of the maze, or where to find Annad. It warned of bleeding, chains, and sorrow, without hope of escape.

Exhaustion mingled with despair flooded over Rowan like a wave. He bowed his head.

As sleep closed around him he heard Allun's voice, tired and angry. "We heard bells when first we came through the door from the Wastelands. But which of us heard them first? The mirror could be the metal walls of this maze. But what is the truth it tells?"

"No doubt we will discover these things in time." Zeel sounded very cold, as though all warm life had been drained out of her. "It has been so with the other prophecies, and so it will be with this."

Allun groaned with weariness. "I am sick of thinking of it. Sleep now, Zeel," he said. "I will wake you in—"

"No," Zeel broke in. "I will take first watch."

Allun yawned. "As you like," Rowan heard him say.

Then there was no sound but the roaring of the pump and the rushing of the water in the pipes. And at last Rowan slept.

He woke, startled, with Perlain's voice in his ear and Perlain's cool hand on his shoulder. He sat up with a jerk, shaking his head, trying to clear his mind.

As his confusion passed, he realized that there was light on his face. The door into the passage was open! He scrambled to his feet as Allun, looking very troubled, came back through the door and closed it behind him.

"No sign?" asked Perlain.

Allun shook his head.

"What is it?" Rowan demanded, bewildered and afraid. "How long have I slept? Why did you not wake me before?"

"I have only just woken myself," said Allun. "Perlain found us both here, sound asleep. But Zeel was not with us, Rowan. She is not outside in the corridor, either. She has gone."

14 ∽ THE HAND MUST BLEED

"Perhaps Zeel heard something and went to see what it was," Rowan suggested weakly.

A feeling of dread was rising in him. Ever since they entered the Zebak city, Zeel had been quiet and strange. Long-buried memories were stirring in her. But it was hard to believe that Zeel—so strong, so long raised in Traveler ways—would be unable to face her past and defeat it.

Unwilling to stand longer in the dark, they opened the door again and cautiously moved out into the bright light. The corridor stretched before them, shining and empty.

Allun shook his head. "What will we do now?" he exclaimed. "If she has ventured alone into this maze of corridors, she will be hopelessly lost by now."

He caught sight of his reflection in the metal wall. His cheek was still streaked with black from the lamp. He rubbed at it crossly, smearing it even more. Then he gave an exclamation and moved closer to the wall.

"There is a smear of black grease on the wall here. And look—there is another, farther along. And another!" He moved along the corridor, pointing out small marks on its shining surface as he went.

Perlain and Rowan hurried after him.

"Zeel had oily soot from the lamp all over her hands," Allun said excitedly. "She used it to leave a trail behind her so that she could find her way back."

"Or so that we could follow," Perlain suggested quietly.

When they reached a place where the corridor was crossed by another, the small black marks continued to the left. They turned the corner and went on.

"This is what Sheba's rhyme meant," Allun gabbled over his shoulder as he led the way. "Though we all heard the bells, I must have been the one who heard them first. So it was I who saw the marks on the mirror and realized that they were signs for us. It is wonderful."

"There has been another prophecy?" asked Perlain. "Tell me."

Rowan repeated the rhyme as they followed Allun around another corner and found themselves in a much broader, longer passage that stretched away on both sides, straight and unbroken.

The Maris man listened intently. "I do not like this talk of chains and sorrow," he said when Rowan had finished. "And the hand that must bleed—I do not like that either. For all of us are the fingers on fate's hand, according to the rhyme Sheba gave you in her hut."

Allun had stopped. When they caught up to him, they saw that all the eagerness had drained from his face. "I am a fool to have rejoiced," he muttered. "For if the first two lines of the verse are true, the rest will be also. Zeel may be in terrible danger now. Why else has she not returned?"

Just then, from somewhere ahead, they heard the sound of many marching feet. They were still distant, but fast coming closer. In seconds the corridor where they stood was echoing with sound.

"They are coming this way!" warned Perlain.

They turned and ran back the way they had come—around the corner where Rowan had told Perlain the rhyme, around the corner before that. There they stopped and listened.

The marching sound was thunderous now.

"Why are we waiting?" whispered Allun. "What if they turn the corner?"

"That is in fate's hands. But judging by the sound, there are many of them," Perlain whispered back. "So with luck they will continue along the broad passage, and we will be safe. We will watch and see. There will still be time to run if they turn."

They peered cautiously around the corner until they could see the place where the broad passage crossed the narrower one.

Left, right, left, right. The pounding came closer, closer. The metal of the wall beside Rowan's face began to tremble.

Then, suddenly, marching Zebak guards came into view. They were four abreast, their gray-clad arms and shining black boots moving in perfect time, their eyes fixed to the front.

Rowan held his breath, poised to run, waiting for them to turn. But they did not turn. They marched straight ahead, as Perlain had predicted they would. Line after line of four passed by as Rowan counted. Six lines . . . eight . . . ten . . . twelve. Then there were no more, and at last the sound faded into the distance.

"Plainly, that broad passage is dangerous," said Allun. "But we must use it if we are to find Zeel. Let us put it behind us as soon as we can."

They went back to the broad passage and began following Zeel's trail once more, half running in their haste, their ears straining for the sound of marching feet. The passage stretched ahead, wide and straight, with no sign of a break until it ended at a sharp turn. If another group of guards appeared, there would be nowhere to hide. They would be seen and captured, as perhaps Zeel had been before them.

But the marks on the wall continued, if less often, and the passage remained empty and silent. They turned the final corner to find themselves in an even broader space that ended in two huge doors with curved metal handles.

They crept up to the doors and listened carefully but could hear no sound.

"Shall we risk it?" whispered Allun.

Perlain shrugged. "We have little choice," he said calmly. He reached for one of the door handles, then hesitated, pointing. Rowan saw that the handle bore a small black smudge, showing that Zeel had touched it.

Perlain pulled the handle, the door swung soundlessly open, and they entered the room beyond.

It was very large and lined with metal cupboards and pegs on which hung Zebak uniforms and caps. A huge table stood in the middle of the room, with benches on either side. There was a great brown flag on the wall, bearing in its center an emblem of black wings like those of the creature that had taken Annad.

"This is where the guards take their rest, if I am not mistaken," said Allun nervously. "It is not a healthy place for us to be."

Across the room was another door. It was partly open, and through the gap they could see a stone wall and the bars of an iron cage.

"Zeel," Rowan said softly. "Perhaps . . ."

They stole across the room and paused at the open door. Again they could hear nothing. But Rowan thought he could feel something. A stirring in the air. A slight, warm breeze that meant that the outside world was near.

They slipped into the stone-walled space beyond the door. Its floor was paved with bricks. Two more doors took up most of one wall, and it was from under those doors that the fresh air came.

Two wheeled cages stood in the center of the space. One, they could see, was empty. The other was partly covered by a cloth. They tiptoed toward it. Allun stretched out his hand to pull away the covering. Cautiously, Rowan bent to see—

And then there was a pounding rush behind him, a heavy weight crashing into his back, a harsh voice ringing in his ears. He yelled and struggled. A powerful hand gripped the back of his neck and drove his head forward into the iron bars of the cage. The world seemed to explode in a blinding flash of light and pain.

"Enough!" thundered a voice. "We want them alive!"

"Yes, sir," growled Rowan's captor.

Rowan was dragged around to face the voice. He could hardly see. His head was spinning, throbbing with pain. He could feel blood trickling down his face. If he had not been held upright, he would have fallen to the ground.

The hand must bleed to reach the end . . .

He became aware that Perlain and Allun were beside him, being held by other rough hands. He could hear Allun groaning. Or was it his own voice he could hear?

Sick and dizzy, he blinked at the tall, gray-uniformed figure striding toward them, heavy black boots ringing on the bricks. By her rigidly straight back and impatient tread he knew that this was a Zebak officer of high rank, without fear or pity. The black line from forehead to nose gave her face a cruel, stern look. Her mouth was set in a harsh line. Her pale eyes were cold under the shining brim of the stiff gray cap with its crest of black wings.

"Silence them, chain them, and put them in the cage," she snapped.

And it was only then, with a shock of horrified disbelief, that Rowan recognized her.

It was Zeel.

15 ～ CHAINS AND
SORROW

Afterward, Rowan realized that he must have fainted as the guard roughly gagged his mouth. When he woke, with a pounding head and a dry throat, he had no idea of how much time had passed. All he knew was that he was lying on the hard floor of the iron cage, chained hand and foot. He could hear Perlain groaning beside him. Probably Allun was on Perlain's other side.

They were prisoners. Prisoners of the Zebak. Zeel had gone to the side of the enemy. Or had she always been there, in her heart? The thought made him feel sick.

Slowly he became aware that the cage was jolting and rocking and that there was a rasping sound of metal wheels rolling over bricks. The cage was being pulled along a road.

The cloth that had been thrown over the cage did not cover it completely. By turning his head a little Rowan could see glimpses of the street through which they were passing.

He saw houses and a baker's wagon. He saw stalls piled with fruit, vegetables, and bags of grain. He saw children playing. He saw adults working or simply walking along carrying baskets, tools, leather bags, babies. All glanced curiously or in a frightened way at the cage, then turned away.

He was surprised to see that they were wearing ordinary clothes, not uniforms. Except for the black stripe from hairline to nose, which all but the very youngest children bore, they did not look very unlike the people at home.

"The cage cover has slipped. Put it right," barked a voice. Rowan's stomach turned over. The voice was Zeel's, but so changed, so cold.

He twisted his head a little more, wincing at the pain, and saw a straight gray back, a swinging arm, and then the side of a stern face, eyes staring straight ahead. Zeel was striding beside the cage. Zeel the betrayer. Zeel, who had used their trust in her to trap them.

One finger stands, the others bend.

"If urks see the prisoners, what does it matter?" growled another voice that Rowan seemed to recognize. "If they know the guards have captured spies inside the city walls, they will understand how dangerous our enemies are. Their discontent will cease. They will understand that the war is necessary for their protection."

"How dare you question my orders?" snapped Zeel. "I told you. This affair is deadly secret! Do as I say!"

"Yes, sir," said the other voice hurriedly.

Rowan suddenly realized that the second speaker was the guard who had complained about having to push the garbage cart. He searched his memory for the name. Zanel. That was it.

The cover was pulled more closely around the cage, and Rowan could see no more. But he could hear. And as he listened, doubt began to stir in his mind. Was it possible that there was something he had not understood? Was it possible . . . ?

"If you and your fellow buffoons had not blundered into this business, you would know nothing about it!" Zeel was saying sternly. "As it happens, I had use for you and decided against reporting you. But beware. I can change my mind at any time, and then it will be the worse for you."

"We were only taking our break, sir," whined Zanel, thoroughly frightened now. "And only early because we had finished our work before time. We did not know the spies were under your guard. They seemed alone and were not chained. What else were we to think but—"

"Silence!" Zeel shouted. "It is not your business to think. Go to the front and urge the beast on. We are moving too slowly."

"I fear this grach cannot move any faster, excuse me, sir," Zanel whimpered. "I had to fetch it from the compound, where it pulls the slaves' plow. Being from Central Control, sir, you are perhaps used to the fighting grach, the ones being trained for the invasion. They are young and strong—and fed on meat from the Wastelands lizards, it is said. But this grach feeds only on grass and scraps. And the compound gate is just ahead."

"These prisoners are to be taken to join the other *without delay*." Zeel's voice was loud and icy cold. "Those are the orders. Do you choose to disobey?"

Plainly, Zanel did not. After a moment Rowan heard his voice at the front of the cage. "Hup! Hup!" he was shouting. The cage lurched as the beast pulling it made a greater effort.

"That is better," Zeel's voice said loudly—so loudly that Rowan was sure she intended the pris-

oners in the cage to hear. "So, very soon our captives will meet their small countrywoman again.
How grateful they must be to have a pleasant ride,
with us to guide their way. Perhaps they feel that
chains and sorrow are not too high a price to pay.
What think you, Zanel?"

> *With chains and sorrow you must pay*
> *For other hands to guide your way.*

The guard walking at the front guffawed at what
he thought was a cruel joke. But Rowan knew that
Zeel's words had been a message. She wanted them
to know that she was having them taken to where
Annad was being kept. And she had used as much as
she dared of Sheba's rhyme to tell them so.

Rowan heard a muffled sound beside him. With
difficulty he turned his head. Perlain's eyes were
wide and excited. He could not speak because of
the gag in his mouth, but Rowan knew that he, too,
had heard Zeel's message and understood.

"Open the gate!" shouted Zeel. "Be quick!"

Rowan felt the cage turn off the brick road and
onto another that seemed to be made of earth. A
gate crashed shut behind them. His body rolled
painfully on the lurching iron floor as the cage rumbled on, but he hardly noticed it. His mind was rac-

ing as he tried to work out what must have happened.

While they slept by the underground lake, Zeel had gone exploring. Somehow, perhaps by following the troop of guards they had seen returning, she had found the place where the uniforms were kept and taken one for herself. She had put it on and used the grease on her fingers to mark her forehead.

Then, perhaps, Zanel and his fellow guards had come in. She hid from them, only showing herself when Rowan, Allun, and Perlain were attacked. She saved her friends from death or capture in the only way she could—by pretending they were already her prisoners.

Now she was continuing to play her part. She was playing it well. And, thanks to her, the problem of how they were going to find Annad had been solved.

There was a shout from the front of the cage, and it stopped with a jolt. "Very well!" Rowan heard Zeel say. "Get them out."

The cover was pulled from the cage. Rowan squinted against the sudden glare of light as slowly, slowly, the world outside the cage came into focus.

He stared, astonished. He had expected to see a prison, with stone or metal walls, iron bars, rows of prisoners in chains. But what he saw were trees,

green fields, a stream, small cottages, people har-
vesting grain. They were so familiar. . . .

A tide of homesickness rose in him, and he wondered wildly if he were dreaming. If a great mountain had towered above the village, if the animals
grazing in the fields had been bukshah instead of
the huge creatures the Zebak called grach, he
would have thought that he was in Rin.

One thing was clear: Annad could not be here.
There had been some sort of mistake. Zeel had
tried her best, and at least they were out of the
maze. But Zanel had brought them to the wrong
place. Perhaps by accident, perhaps not.

The side of the cage opened with a clang. Zanel
reached in and pulled Rowan out like a sack of
grain, then threw him to the ground.

"Take more care," shouted Zeel. "They are not to
be injured. Those are the orders."

Zanel grunted angrily, but heaved Perlain and
Allun out of the cage with more care. They lay on
the ground next to Rowan, unmoving. Rowan stole
a glance at the grach that had pulled the cage. It
had lowered its head and was tearing eagerly at the
grass. It was glad the journey had ended, and it was
home.

"You may go now," Zeel told Zanel severely. "And
remember, you are forbidden to speak of this mat-

ter. If I hear that you have done so you will find yourself outside the wall with the ishkin."

"Yes, sir," mumbled Zanel. He turned to go.

"Wait!" Zeel commanded. "Give me the key to the prisoners' chains. I may need it."

A strange expression crossed Zanel's face. It was surprise, quickly followed by suspicion. "But Central Control guards like yourself have keys to open any lock, sir," he said.

Rowan held his breath. Zeel had made a mistake.

Zeel straightened her shoulders. "I choose to have *your* key, Zanel," she snapped. "Give it to me!"

Zanel stared. Then he took a key from his pocket and walked toward Zeel. She waited, unmoving.

She does not want to seem too eager, Rowan thought. She knows he is suspicious. He strained his wrists against his chains, but he was held fast. There was nothing he could do.

Zanel was very near Zeel now. He peered at her, and his eyes narrowed. She held out her hand for the key.

He took another step and then pretended to trip. His hand flew up, grazed Zeel's forehead, and knocked off her cap. The black line that ran between her nose and hairline smeared into a black smudge. Her long hair fell to her shoulders.

For a single moment Zanel goggled at her, and at

his own hand, which was marked with black grease. Then he gave a roar, drew his dagger, and sprang.

Zeel tried to leap away from him, but the heavy boots and stiff uniform hampered her and she tripped and fell. Watching helplessly, unable even to cry out, Rowan moaned with horror as Zanel lunged for her again, grinning with triumphant rage.

And then, as though by magic, the tall figure of a stranger suddenly plunged toward Zanel from behind the empty cage. He seemed to have appeared from nowhere. He must have crept up on them unseen and stayed hidden till now.

He had fair hair touched with ginger, and he was young—not much more than a boy. He was wearing rough working clothes and carried a garden shovel. But his face was full of a hero's determination; his shoulders were broad and his arms were powerful. With a shout he raised the shovel and brought it crashing down. The next moment, Zanel was lying unconscious on the ground.

His attacker stood panting above him, kicked him gently to see if he would stir, and then seemed satisfied. He picked up the dagger and looked at Rowan, Perlain, and Allun lying helpless on the grass. And at Zeel, scrambling to her feet.

"I am Norris," he said soberly. He leaned on the

shovel as his eyes scanned them one by one, lingering with curiosity on Perlain. Then he turned his gaze back to Rowan, and his face broke into a smile.

"You are welcome, Rowan," he said. "We have been waiting for you."

16 ⌒ SURPRISES

Dumbfounded, Rowan stared at Zeel's rescuer. His first thought was that Norris looked very like Strong Jonn, though he was much younger—still under twenty years, by his broad, smooth face.

Keeping her eyes on Norris, still not sure of him, Zeel bent to unlock Rowan's chains. As she moved on to Allun and Perlain, Rowan sat up and with relief tore the stifling gag from his mouth.

"How do you know my name?" he asked huskily.

Just then the grach, which had quietly gone back to eating grass, raised its head and gave a grunt of pleasure. Rowan looked behind him and saw that an old man with long white hair and beard was hobbling toward them from one of the cottages. He was small and thin, and looked very worried.

"Oh, Norris!" He sighed as he reached them.
"Again you have acted without thinking and used
your strength instead of your wits. My poor boy,
what am I to do with you?" As he spoke, he fondled
the grach, which had lumbered up to him, dragging
the empty cage.

Norris's face flushed, and he hung his head. It was
clear that he felt clumsy and shamed. Rowan was
sorry for him. He well understood what it was to be
a disappointment to others. How often had he felt
it himself? But for entirely the opposite reason.

Zeel stepped forward. "Norris saved my life, old
one," she said firmly. "He had no choice but to
attack. What else was he to do?"

The old man shook his head. Plainly he could
think of nothing, but he stared at Zanel's unconscious body with dismay.

"They will come looking for the poor creature,"
he said at last in his gentle, hesitating voice. "We
must hide him—and the cage, too. Under the
haystack behind the cottage, perhaps. And then we
will think what we should do."

He sighed again as Norris roughly dumped the
guard into the cage and crashed the door shut.
Then he seemed to remember the watching
strangers. He turned to Rowan and bowed.

"Greetings, Rowan," he said. "Forgive our squabbling. Poor Norris is a good-hearted boy, but his hasty ways drive me to despair. I am Thiery of the Silk. My home is yours."

Before Rowan could answer, Thiery had turned to Allun, Zeel, and Perlain. "I am pleased and interested to meet you," he said. "We were expecting Rowan, but no others."

He turned and began to walk slowly back to his cottage. With Norris at its side, the grach followed, pulling the cage behind it.

"Why were you expecting me?" Rowan burst out, stumbling after them.

"Your sister told us you would come," Thiery said simply.

"Annad!" Rowan's heart leaped. "She *is* here!"

Thiery looked mildly surprised. "Of course. Where else would they put a new slave?"

"We thought she would be in a prison," said Perlain. By his polite voice and veiled eyes Rowan could see that he thought the old man was either simple-minded or not to be trusted.

Thiery stopped. "This *is* a prison, my friend," he said. "In the compound we are prisoners of the Zebak as surely as if we were in iron cages." He lifted his stick and swung it so that its tip pointed out for them the high wire fence that stretched around the green fields.

Zeel turned to look at the distant workers and frowned. "But those people are Zebak," she said sharply. "I see their brow marks."

"Oh, yes," agreed Thiery. "Ordinary Zebak folk—those the guards call 'urks'—come to the compound each day to join us in the fields. It has been many years since there have been enough slaves to do the work alone."

He glanced at Zeel. "You, too, are Zebak," he said. "But where is *your* brow mark?"

Zeel lifted her chin proudly. "I became the daughter of another land when I was very young," she answered. "These clothes I put on only to deceive the guards."

Rowan felt a snuffling at his shoulder, and without thinking he put up his hand. When his fingers felt scaly skin instead of warm wool, he jerked his hand away. But then the grach moaned in disappointment, so he put his hand back. If any creature wanted comfort, he could not deny it, however fearsome its appearance.

"The prophecy we were given said that the one who first heard Zebak bells should use the truth the mirror told," Zeel was explaining. "I heard the bells long ago, as a tiny child. And my reflection in the walls had made me face the truth that I was Zebak, however much I pretended I was not. Suddenly I saw how I, and I alone, could take us forward. It was my turn to play my part. As Perlain played his on the sea, and Allun in the Wastelands."

"The Wastelands!" gasped Norris, eyeing them with new respect.

"And what will Rowan's part be, I wonder?" asked Thiery.

His voice was very quiet. Rowan looked away from the grach and met Thiery's eyes. He thought he saw great sadness there, and wondered. But the old man quickly turned to Zeel again.

"Coming to the city must have been painful for you," he said gently.

"Yes," Zeel admitted in a low voice. "I felt that my friends must hate me for my birth. I hated myself."

So *that* was why Zeel had seemed so cold and withdrawn in the maze, thought Rowan, putting his hand on her arm.

"*Hate* you, Zeel?" Allun was exclaiming at the same time.

"It is not your fault that this land is at war with ours and its people are cruel," added Perlain quietly.

As Zeel's troubled face warmed, Norris shuffled his feet. "We should move on," he warned them. He was clearly embarrassed by this show of feeling. Again he reminded Rowan vividly of Jonn. And of

Jiller, too, and even of little Annad. All of them would understand Norris's nature in a way that Thiery could not.

Norris is a stranger to his own people, as I am to mine, Rowan thought, as they began to walk again, matching their strides to the old man's slow steps.

The cottages were now not far ahead, and Rowan noticed for the first time that all but the one from which Thiery had come were in ruins. Their roofs were full of holes, their doors sagged open, and their windows were broken.

He wanted to ask Thiery about this, but the old man had been thinking about Perlain's last words and was speaking again.

"The Zebak people are not cruel by nature," he said, shaking his head. "Most are a little stern, but that is all. The guards are the cruel ones. They use their whips and their boots freely to show their power. Many ordinary folk would escape the land if they could. But the sea, their path to freedom, has been forbidden to them for many years now."

He turned to Zeel. "Your parents must have been among the last to attempt to flee by boat," he said gently. "If they paid for it with their lives, their action gave you, at least, a chance for a new life."

Zeel lowered her head.

"The people are prisoners in their city, as we are in the compound," Thiery went on. "The city walls are high, and the wings of the working grach are clipped each year so they cannot fly." He pressed his lips together. "It gives the beasts great pain," he added, as if this hurt him almost more than anything.

"The guards are all-powerful," Norris growled, glaring at the still figure inside the cage with hatred. "The people are helpless against them."

"But this is changing," Thiery said. "I feel it. The tide is turning."

He threw open the cottage door, ignoring Norris's snort of disbelief. Rowan walked from the hot sun into the pleasant coolness within and stopped short.

Despite his eagerness to see Annad, for a moment all he could do was look around, wondering why he felt so instantly at home. In size and shape, it was true, the room was like the living rooms in Rin. But instead of being plain and containing only those things that were useful, this room was full of light and bright colors.

Long blue curtains were pulled back from the large windows. There was a beautiful patterned rug on the floor, and paintings hung on the walls. The couch was heaped with embroidered cushions. On the shelf above the fireplace stood a yellow jug of flowers.

"My granddaughter's work, and mine," Thiery's gentle voice murmured. "I am glad you find it pleasing. But you will want to see your sister. . . ."

With a guilty start Rowan turned and followed him up the narrow stairs to the attic. Perlain, Allun, and Zeel crowded behind.

"All is well, Shaaran," Thiery called as he entered a small bedroom.

There, on a narrow bed under a spread embroidered with leaves and flowers, lay Annad, fast asleep. The fragrant scent of sweet herbs drifted on the air.

A slim, dark-haired girl was standing beside the bed with her hand on the back of a chair. Her soft eyes were startled. She still clutched an open book, as if she had jumped up in fright on hearing their footsteps.

"The child's brother has come," Thiery told her, ushering Rowan into the room. "Rowan, this is my granddaughter, Shaaran."

The girl was about Rowan's age, but no taller than he was. She smiled shyly in greeting, and to his astonishment Rowan was filled with the feeling that he had met her before. That is impossible, he told himself. But the feeling was strong and would not leave him.

"I am glad you are here," Shaaran was saying. "Annad has slept for almost all the time she has been with us, but whenever she stirred she said your name."

While his friends waited at the door, Rowan tiptoed to the bed. Annad was pale and there were some scratches on her face, but she was breathing peacefully. His heart swelled with relief.

As he looked down at her, her eyes flickered, then opened. She stared up at him without the least surprise, and smiled. "I knew you would come for me, Rowan." She sighed. "I was not afraid."

Rowan smiled back at her. "You are never afraid," he said. He bent over her, and the medallion hanging around his neck swung free. He heard a gasp from behind him, but he could not turn to look because Annad's fingers had caught the medallion and held it fast.

"Pretty," she said, and yawned widely.

"Sleep again now, Annad," Rowan said. "I will be here when you wake."

Annad nodded drowsily. "And you will take me home," she said. Her eyelids were already growing heavy again. She blinked at Shaaran. "My brother is a great hero, you know," she murmured. Then her eyes closed, the fingers clutching the medallion loosened, and she fell back to sleep.

Rowan straightened and stepped away from the bed. His heart was very full. Home? Would any of them ever see home again? He turned, anxious to know what had caused the gasp he had heard.

Shaaran had put her arm around her grandfather's shoulders. To his surprise, Rowan saw that the old man's faded eyes were glistening with tears.

"I knew you would come one day," he said, his voice quavering. "I believed, as my father before me. As our family has always believed. And so we went on, painting the silks for you, as slowly we faded away. . . ."

Rowan stared at him, confused and a little afraid. Was Thiery mad? He looked helplessly at Shaaran and saw that she was trembling.

"Grandfather, Rowan does not understand," she whispered to the old man. She looked back at Rowan. "When Annad came, we wondered if at last the time had come," she said. "Her face—her strength—"

She broke off, swallowing desperately to hold back her tears. "We hoped—could not be certain," she went on. "And then—just now—to see the medallion, and know . . . It is a great happiness for Grandfather, and for me. But a great shock also."

Rowan shook his head. He felt dazed. "What—what is this place?" he stammered. "Who are you?"

"We are your people, Rowan," Shaaran said softly. "All that are left. And this is your place. This is Rin."

17 ∾ PAINTED SHADOWS

"You are not my people! I have never seen you before this day. And this is not Rin! Rin is far away, across the sea!" The words burst from Rowan almost angrily. Shaaran shrank back, looking to her grandfather for help, very aware of Allun, Perlain, and Zeel clustered just inside the door, their faces startled.

"They called their new home after their old, Shaaran," the old man murmured. "Their memories had been taken from them, but the name came to them and they used it, without knowing why."

"Who?" Rowan demanded. "Who are you talking about?" He found that he was shaking.

"Your ancestors," Thiery said. "The strong ones who left us over three hundred years ago and never returned."

Rowan stared, openmouthed.

Thiery smiled wearily and slumped down on the chair beside Annad's bed. "I am very tired. You must show him, Shaaran, my dear. I will watch over the child."

Shaaran was plainly worried about him, but obediently she beckoned to Rowan and together they followed Zeel, Allun, and Perlain down the narrow stairs. Shaaran took a folded sheet from a cupboard. Then she led them out the back door of the cottage and into the open air.

Beyond the vegetable garden a large haystack stood. Norris was forking hay over the iron cage, which was already almost completely covered.

The grach grazed peacefully nearby. It looked up as they came out, but when it saw that Thiery was not with them, it lost interest and went back to its feeding.

The friends followed Shaaran down some stone steps that led to a cellar below the cottage. Inside, it was as dark and cold as the grave, but the girl lit a candle. Bundles of root vegetables and a stack of firewood came into view. The light flickered eerily on walls and floor. Shadows were flat black monsters crawling on the stones.

Shaaran took a pointed iron bar from its place against the wall, carried it to the room's darkest corner, and stuck it into a gap between the cornerstone and the wall. Seeing what she was trying to do, Zeel and Allun went to her aid, adding their weight to the bar so that the stone was raised.

Beneath it was a dark hole.

Shaaran thrust her arm inside it and drew out a chain that was attached to a hook somewhere near the top. She pulled, and soon a large box swung into view, dangling from the end of the chain like a fish on a line.

She placed the box on the floor and opened it. Inside were dozens of thin rolls of silk. Each roll was as wide as Rowan's arm was long, and each was tied with a braided cord like the one he now wore around his neck. Some of the rolls looked newer than others. Some were very old indeed.

"What are they?" Allun burst out, craning his neck to see.

"Our story," Shaaran said. "I will show you."

She spread the sheet on the dusty floor. Then she unrolled the long pieces of silk upon it, one by one, starting with the oldest.

In the flickering candlelight, painted figures and scenes seemed to leap up at them from the silken backgrounds. Clear, bright colors brought to glowing life a time long gone. This village, full of people and sturdy cottages. Men, women, and children

working in the fields. Mottled grach pulling plows
and carts. Zebak guards, chains, iron cages . . .

Rowan's hand burned.

The painted shadows live again. . . .

Each silk told a different story. And all the stories
put together made a longer tale—a sad and terrible
tale that had been three hundred years in the
telling.

"Long ago, Rowan, our people were one,"
Shaaran said, her hand moving over the oldest silks.
"We had been slaves of the Zebak so long that our
old history had been lost, for the Zebak had killed
anyone who mentioned times past. We worked in
the fields, growing food for the city. There were
many of us—brave and timid, strong and weak,
those who could paint and sew and heal the sick—
and those who could climb and run and fight."

She was repeating a lesson she had learned long
ago, and the words came easily. But her eyes were
sad, as though for the moment she was living in the
past, and grieved.

"Three hundred years ago the Zebak leaders
made a great plan to invade a land across the sea,"
she went on. "They had fought the people of that
land before and knew they would defend themselves with all their strength. Many Zebak would
die. So they decided to add to their forces. They

took the strongest and bravest of us away to be trained as warriors and sacrificed to the cause. . . ."

Such was the roaring in his ears that Rowan could hardly hear her voice as it continued. And he did not need to. One painting showed the story all too clearly.

It showed guards rounding up people from the village and putting them into iron cages to which grach were harnessed. It showed the weeping and pain as sons and daughters were torn away from their mothers, brother was separated from brother, husband from wife.

The ones who were being taken were tall and strong. They reminded him of his family, the people he knew at home, and Norris. The ones who were being left behind were smaller and weaker looking—of no use as warriors. They were like Shaaran. Like Thiery. Like himself.

Shaaran's slim finger pointed to a bent old woman standing close to one of the iron cages. She carried a bundle of herbs, to show that she was a wise woman and a healer. She was secretly passing something through the bars of the cage to another, much younger, woman inside.

Rowan bent closer to see what the object was and when he saw, he gasped. It was a medallion on a braided silk cord.

"It is the same," Shaaran said. "You are wearing it now. It has been passed down through the generations for three hundred years, and now it has returned. We have always believed that one day it would."

"So you knew that the warrior slaves did not die," Rowan said slowly. "You knew they turned against the Zebak and helped to defeat them."

Shaaran nodded, pointing to the next piece of silk which showed vivid scenes of battle. The Zebak were being driven back into the sea by their own strong slaves. With the slaves were the Maris, who had been painted with fish tails, and the Travelers, wild with feathers and fierce, laughing faces.

Perlain snorted. "The Maris do not have tails," he said stiffly.

"Neither do the Travelers look quite so much like devils as this, I hope." Zeel smiled.

"My ancestors could not paint truly what they had never seen," said Shaaran apologetically. "They had to rely upon the tales they heard when the Zebak who had survived came limping home. That is how they heard that their lost people had remained in the new land."

"And happily forgotten the loved ones they had left behind in slavery!" Allun's voice was harsh.

"Do not judge them, Allun," said Rowan quietly.

"The Zebak have ways of controlling minds, and plainly it has always been so. They washed their warrior slaves' memories clean, so that they would fight well and not pine for their loved ones."

Shaaran nodded. "That is why my ancestors took a great risk and began painting the silks. So that if ever the lost ones returned to this land, they might find them and learn their story—even if there was no one left to tell it."

Her voice was very quiet as she said these last words. Rowan looked at the remaining silk strips. They showed the people working as before, but even harder, and in greater sadness. They showed guards taking young ones who showed any sign of rebellion and throwing them into the Wastelands. They showed overgrown fields, and houses gradually falling down. They showed adults growing older and dying, but fewer and fewer children being born to take their places. They showed Zebak people being brought in to do their work, so that there would still be food for the city. The very last showed three figures only. Two children and an old man, standing alone by a grave.

When pain is truth and truth is pain . . .

"My parents had children only because our family had always painted the silks, and they wished the work to go on for as long as possible," Shaaran said.

"They could see from the first that Norris—was not suitable. So they had me. But we are the last."

So Thiery, Norris, and Shaaran were all that were left of these quiet, gentle people. They had preferred to waste away rather than to go on bearing children in slavery.

Rowan understood. He would have felt the same way. He understood, too, at last, why he was different from others in his village, and why there had been others like him in the past.

The people of Rin had forgotten the loved ones they had left behind, but nature had not. Now and again, like black bukshah calves, oddities were born. Oddities like him, who took after a side of the Rin family that none of them had known existed.

"Grandfather painted this silk after our parents died of fever, seven years ago," Shaaran was saying. "He has painted no more since. He has not had the heart, and there has been nothing to tell."

"Well, there is something now," said Zeel fiercely.

"There is," Allun agreed. "But I do not think we can wait for painting. This place is dangerous for us. Perlain is already impatient. I can see it by the way he lashes his tail."

Shaaran laughed out loud, then bit her lip and glanced at Perlain to see if he was insulted. But Perlain simply smiled coolly.

"I am indeed impatient," he said. "And if I *did* have a tail, it would be lashing like a serpent. We must find a way of leaving here as soon as we can. But we will need help."

"Norris and I will help you," Shaaran offered eagerly. "We have trusted friends among the people who work in the fields. And when the guards come, we can delay them while you—"

"No, Shaaran!" Rowan broke in. "We are not going alone. You are coming with us."

She stared at him, astounded. "We cannot go," she whispered. "The guards will not let us go."

"They will not let *us* go, either, if they can help it," Rowan said as cheerfully as he could. "Pack away the silks. We will not leave them behind."

Shaaran turned away and began to roll the silk strips, her fingers trembling.

"Rowan!" Perlain's face was very grave, and Rowan knew what he was thinking. They had survived so far by a miracle. Their way from here would be doubly hard. Hampered by four more people, including a small child, a timid girl, and a frail old man, how could they survive?

But Rowan knew he could not leave them. He fumbled in his shirt for Sheba's oilcloth package, drew out a stick and plunged it into the candle flame.

Green light leaping on the stone walls, on the motionless figures of his friends, on Shaaran's startled face, on the rolls of silk. Burning pain. Sheba's face, grinning at him . . .

> *When evil strikes and fury wakes,*
> *Then love will face the choice it makes.*
> *Death will free the loyal friend.*
> *As it began, so will it end.*
> *Bound to the beast, you play your part—*
> *The comfort of the aching heart.*

Struggling against the wave of tiredness and despair that was engulfing him, Rowan repeated the words. His friends said nothing, for what was there to say?

Yet surely the rhyme's meaning could not be what it seemed.

"It does not mean that we have only death and slavery before us," he muttered at last. "It *cannot* mean that."

"Sheba did warn us," said Allun, his lips twisted in a bitter smile.

Rowan knew that he was thinking of the words that had haunted them all from the beginning, though they had never spoken of them.

Five leave, but five do not return. . . .

Shaaran looked down at the evil-smelling oil-cloth lying tangled on the cellar floor. All that remained of its contents were a sorry handful of limp, pale grass and a single stick.

"There—there is one stick left," she stammered. "Does this not mean that it is too soon to give up hope?"

Rowan glanced at her quickly. Her pale face showed her fear, but she was fighting the fear with all her strength. She would not give way to it.

And neither would he.

"You are right," he said, folding up the cloth and putting it back inside his shirt. "The story is not yet finished."

Heavy feet thumped on the cellar steps. Then Norris swung through the door, carrying Annad, sleepy and blinking, in his arms. "Guards are marching toward the compound," he called urgently. "The people will delay them at the gate, but you must make haste. If they find you here, they will kill us all!"

18 ∾ AS IT BEGAN . . .

Outside, Thiery was waiting for them, his face filled with alarm. The grach hissed anxiously beside him, and he stroked its neck, trying to soothe it, as the friends quickly discussed what they should do.

"We cannot face the Wastelands again," Allun said firmly. "That is certain."

"The prophecy said, 'As it began, so will it end,'" said Perlain. "Our journey began on the sea. We must try to get to the shore and steal a boat."

"If only I had not been forced to leave my kite behind when I changed my clothes!" Zeel shook her head angrily, then swung around to Norris. "Can you show us the quickest way to the shore?"

"I could," said Norris grimly, "but it would not help you. The wall circles the city. The Wastelands are the one place where the doors are not heavily guarded day and night. And in any case, the shore is ringed by spiked wire that cannot be crossed."

"But surely—" Allun began.

Norris's face flushed with anger. "If escape were as easy as you seem to suppose, we ourselves would have done it," he shouted. He looked around at them, his fists clenched. "I am not a coward or a fool. Do you think I wish to remain here in slavery?"

Thiery sighed at his grandson's anger. But the visitors well understood it. It was the anger that any ordinary citizen of Rin would have showed in Norris's shoes.

"No one doubts your courage or your sense, friend," Perlain said calmly. "But we are with you now. This makes a difference."

"Oh?" jeered Norris. "And why is that?"

"Because if we *can* escape the city, we at least know where we can sail to reach safety," Rowan said.

"Safety?" Norris scowled. "There is no safety in your land. Do you not understand? The test that brought your sister here proved to the Zebak that an attack from the air will succeed. They are wasting no more time. Even now, it is said, the grach fleet is massing in the great square, preparing to leave. Soon your land will be invaded and overcome."

"Our land will *not* be overcome," said Zeel firmly. "Our people will fight."

Norris shook his head. "Nothing can defeat the fighting grach. Their skins are as tough as iron, and their claws, teeth, and tails can kill with ease."

"And yet your grach is so gentle." Rowan looked at the huge creature snuffling lovingly at Thiery's hand.

Norris shrugged impatiently. "Unos is a working grach. The fighting grach have been specially bred for war. They learn to seek the scent of a beast that lives only in your land. The trainers have the hide of one such beast, brought back by the survivors of what they call the War of the Plains."

"But the War of the Plains was long ago!" Allun exclaimed.

"Invasion by air has been Central Control's treasured plan for many years," Norris said. "It has cost much in supplies and labor. The people do not like it, but they are told it must be done for their own safety."

"That is a lie," said Perlain flatly. "We fight only to defend ourselves."

"Already the people know this, in their hearts." Thiery nodded, gazing over the fields. "For long ages their labor and their lives have been wasted in making useless war. Their anger is growing strong enough to overcome their fear of disobedience. They whisper of rebellion."

"But that is why Central Control is determined that this invasion will succeed, Grandfather," growled Norris. "The leaders believe that new land to settle and fresh slaves to work in the fields will stop the protest."

Rowan felt a chill of fear, then jumped as he heard distant shouts. The guards had reached the compound gates.

"We must leave at once," said Allun abruptly. "Norris—will you lead us to the shore, or not?"

Norris hesitated.

"If Norris will not do it, I will."

Everyone turned in surprise, for it was Shaaran who had spoken. She had been so quiet that they had almost forgotten about her. Her face burned, but she met their eyes determinedly.

"I, too, know the way," she said.

"No, Shaaran!" wailed the old man, and Unos the grach moaned softly, feeling her master's fear.

"It would be a useless waste of life. There is no escape by sea," Norris said stubbornly.

"This is our one chance at freedom, Norris!" cried Shaaran. "Let us take it!"

The old man paused, looking from one to the other. Then, strangely, he smiled. He bent to kiss

Shaaran's brow, and put a gentle hand on Norris's shoulder. "You are both right, my dears," he murmured. "Forgive me. For a moment I wavered. Fear has always been my enemy. You have both taught me to be strong."

He raised his hand to stroke Unos again, then turned away and began hurrying toward the haystack. "Before anything can be done, I must see to the injured guard," he called back over his shoulder. "He will by now have woken."

"The old fool is mad!" exploded Zeel.

"We cannot wait," muttered Perlain. "We will have to leave him."

"No!" Norris exclaimed.

"Grandfather," called Shaaran, thrusting the box of silks into Rowan's arms and running after the old man. "Grandfather, we must go!"

"Stay back, Shaaran," shouted Thiery, tearing at the hay, strewing it everywhere. "This is my task!"

Unos had spread her wings and was half lumbering, half flapping after her master like some great bird trying to protect its chick.

Suddenly Rowan realized something. He spun around to Norris.

"Your grach's wings—they have not been clipped!" he exclaimed.

"No. For many years Grandfather has bribed our

guards to spare Unos, by giving them extra food," Norris answered gruffly. "He gave his word that while he lived he would not let her fly, so that Central Control would never know."

Rowan's thoughts were racing. A grach had stolen Annad, flown away with her. *That* was the beginning. And a grach's flight could be the end.

"Unos is big enough to take all of us," he cried. "We could—"

Norris shook his head, watching the old man. "Grandfather gave his word," he said sulkily. "He will never break it. Not even—"

Then, suddenly, his eyes widened, and at the same moment Rowan heard Shaaran cry out.

A dark figure was leaping from within the haystack. Zanel had freed himself from the cage. He had been hiding, waiting. . . .

"Slave! Traitor!" he shouted, his face twisted with rage. "Do you dare to imprison *me!*" He seized Thiery, shaking him like a child's cloth doll. Then the blade of a dagger flashed in the sunlight as he raised it and plunged it into the old man's heart.

Shaaran screamed, running forward as Thiery crumpled and fell. Zanel seized her in her turn, and she screamed again. Rowan, Norris, Allun, Perlain and Zeel were shouting as they leaped to help her. But their cries were drowned by another sound—a terrible, animal wail of pain as Unos mourned her master.

"Stay back!" Zanel shouted, the dagger held high in his hand. "I will kill the girl if you move."

They stopped, eyeing him warily.

"Fools!" he snarled. "Did you think I would carry just one weapon? Did you think a lock would keep me in a cage when the dagger in my boot could break it? Lie down. Now! Flat on your bellies in the dust where you belong. Or the girl will suffer for it."

Grimly, the friends glanced at one another.

"Go! Run!" sobbed Shaaran, as she struggled against the guard's strong arm. Tears were streaming down her face, but she shook her head violently. "Please! It does not matter about me! Go now!"

Zanel tightened his grip around her neck, strangling her cries. Lifting her off her feet with ease, he dragged her forward, stepping over Thiery's body, kicking at it carelessly.

The grach looked up from her grieving. Her flat yellow eyes burned, and she hissed deep in her throat as she looked at the man who had killed her master.

Zanel looked around in surprise. To him, grach had always been simple beasts of burden, to be used, like slaves, without respect and certainly without fear. But never had he seen animal eyes so full of hatred.

Fear flickered across his face. "Down, grach!" he said uncertainly.

Unos bared her teeth. Her forked tongue flickered out, tasting her enemy's fear. The spines on her neck rose and stood upright. Her whole body seemed swollen as she moved slowly toward Zanel, spreading her huge wings.

"Down!" shrieked Zanel, backing away. He slashed at her pointlessly with the dagger that had killed an old man but that against this terrible foe was as useless as a toy. Then suddenly he turned, cast Shaaran aside, and began to run.

The grach paused in midstep. At first, hardly daring to watch, Rowan thought she was going to let the guard go. Then, as he was almost away, the divided tail flicked. Like three whips spiked with thorns, it struck with casual, deadly force. Zanel screamed once. But by the time he hit the ground, he breathed no more.

Rowan was shaking with the horror of what he had seen. He could hear Shaaran weeping, Allun cursing, and Annad calling to him. But as he watched Unos lumbering back to them, her strong, leathery wings trailing in the dust behind her, the fire of anger in her eyes dying back to dull sadness, he remembered Sheba's words.

When evil strikes and fury wakes,
Then love will face the choice it makes.
Death will free the loyal friend.
As it began, so will it end.

With a heavy heart he moved to Shaaran's side. "Do not weep," he said gently. "Your grandfather died as he wished. He made his choice. His oath died with him, so his loyal friend is free to fly again. And as he planned, she will take us home."

19 ⌒ . . . SO WILL IT END

The grach flew west, following the scent. She had flown for a long time, and she was tired and hungry, but the boy's gentle voice and stroking hands gave her the strength to go on. There was little thought behind her flat yellow eyes. Just one fixed idea. She must follow the scent, reach the place she had been told to reach, and deliver her riders to the place they wanted to go.

The sea had been left behind long ago, and dimly the grach was aware that below her now were rolling green hills and a winding stream of water, glinting bright in the sunlight. She was aware that a mountain, its peak hidden in cloud, rose in the blue distance ahead.

But her eyes were not important. Her ears, closed against the rushing of the wind, the beating of her aching wings, were not important, either. All that was important was her forked tongue, flickering in and out, tasting the cold air, tasting the scent.

She knew she was close to her goal. The scent was stronger—the good smell of dust, fire, ash, and bitter herbs that made her jaws drip with hunger. Sheba. She even knew the name.

"Sheba," the gentle boy had said, flourishing the small oilcloth bundle in front of her face, feeding her the limp stems of pale grass from inside it so that their delicious sweet-sour taste mingled with the smell. When her riders had climbed upon her back and tied themselves in place, the boy had said it again. "Sheba. Seek."

And then the grach had spread her wings and flown. Over the empty, ruined cottages and the fields where workers looked up, waving and cheering, and a troop of guards shouted. Over the city with its flaming tower, its gathered army of fighting grach, its gray-clad figures pointing, running. Then on over the gleaming wall, over the burning Wastelands, over churning sea, over jagged cliffs, and on to this green land.

The Sheba scent was strong. The scents of grach and Zebak were strong, too, and growing stronger. But there were other scents. Some of these Unos had tasted before. Two she had not. One of those she had not tasted was a warm, animal smell. There was no threat in it. But the other was full of danger. It was fire, snow, and ice. It was hot breath, dripping fangs, and ancient, jealous power.

The leathery spines on the grach's back prickled with warning. But the boy's soothing voice was soft in her ear, so her yellow lizard eyes did not flicker and the beating of her scaly mottled wings did not falter as she flew on, to Rin.

Star scanned the blue, blue sky above the village. It was still clear, except for the cloud that always shrouded the tip of the forbidden Mountain, and two kites, one white, one red, riding the wind. And yet—surely there was something in the sky to fear. Something to fear—but something to welcome, also. The scents were mixed. Good and evil. Coming closer.

She had already taken the herd to the lowest part of the field, beyond the drinking pool. Now she began to lead them into a circle. It was time. The birds had hidden long ago. She could hear shouting in the village. She could see people with weapons and flaming torches. Beyond the village she could see Ogden the Traveler standing on a hill like a tree against the sky, watching the kites and listening, listening.

But her duty was to the herd. To protect the calves, to hold the circle. She stood as still as a statue in her place, sniffing the air. She was ready. She had done what she could.

"We cannot be sure where the creatures will land!" Solla the sweets maker, plump and soft, waddled, panting, toward the bukshah field. He clutched his quickly sharpened spear tightly while his eyes darted to and fro.

"We cannot be sure," snapped old Lann, hobbling beside him. "That is why the Travelers guard the hills, and why I have left some forces in the square. But if the beasts have been trained to follow the bukshah scent, as Timon believes, they will land at the field."

She was leaning heavily on her stick, but in her other hand she, too, carried a spear. It was her own, and she had sharpened it with her own hands. Once she had been Rin's greatest fighter, and she was determined that age would not prevent her from again defending her home—with her life, if fate so willed.

She stopped to rest, her keen old eyes searching the sky. She made out the tiny figures of Tor and Mithren dangling unprotected beneath their kites, watching for the first sight of the enemy. Her warrior's heart thrilled at their courage. She wondered at how often she had jibed at the Travelers for their lighthearted, wandering ways.

I had forgotten, she thought. I fought beside Travelers, and Maris, too, in the War of the Plains. I of all here should have remembered their worth. But time passed, and I forgot.

She glanced at Bronden the furniture maker, who had stopped beside her. Bronden, too, was looking up, her face haggard. Lann knew that she had not slept since the day Annad was taken and Rowan of the Bukshah, Perlain of Pandellis, Allun the baker, and Zeel of the Travelers had left in pursuit.

It had not been what Bronden expected—that the despised ones, the oddities, should do what she herself would never dare. It had shaken her to her core.

Lann saw Bronden's eyes widen, and she looked upward. The kites were dipping, plunging, like waterbirds ducking for fish. And on the silent hill Ogden was raising his arms.

The enemy was coming.

Lann's mouth set into a firm, hard line. She grasped her spear more tightly and set off for the bukshah field once more.

Bronden strode beside her, stocky and strong. When she spoke, her voice was harsh and grating.

"They will not take us," she said. "Our people will not be slaves again. We will die first."

"Let us not think of dying," Lann answered coolly. "Only of winning."

Her words were the words of a leader, but her heart was heavy as she reached the field and saw her people gathered, waiting. They were brave and determined, but they were few. And of what use were their weapons against the creatures they were about to face?

At the front, towering above the rest, stood Strong Jonn. Beside him were Jiller and Marlie the weaver, both holding bows and arrows.

These three seemed apart from the crowd. They were pale, and their faces bore the marks of great grief. But grimly they stood together, shoulder to shoulder. For them, this battle would be for revenge as well as for freedom.

Lann pushed her way through the people until she reached them.

"Did you see Sheba?" she shouted. "Did she speak?"

Jiller shook her head. "It was as before," she said evenly. "She has not moved. Specks of ash have settled on her face, and a spider has spun a web across her chair. The fire was burning green and would not let us near her."

Lann frowned. "Is it illness? Trance?"

"Whatever it may be, she did not stir, however loudly we called," said Jiller. "Her eyes are closed. Yet she breathes. It is as though her spirit has left her body."

"There!" Jonn shouted, pointing upward. "Look there!"

A black speck could be seen against the pale blue of the horizon. It was growing larger by the second. The kites wheeled and sped toward it.

"Only one!" someone in the crowd called in relief.

"The same, perhaps, come for another child," cried another voice. "Well, we are ready for it this time."

Jonn shook his head. "Ogden said he felt a great menace," he muttered. "Far greater than before. If there is only one, it must be the first of many."

They watched, transfixed, as the black shape grew larger, larger. Now they could see its great wings beating the air. The kites swooped and darted around it, and it seemed to fall lower in the sky.

"They are worrying it," said Jonn with grim satisfaction.

Marlie spoke for the first time. "I see shapes upon its back," she said. "It has riders."

Jiller raised her pale face and squared her shoulders, slowly fitting an arrow to her bow.

"Kites!" Annad squealed to Rowan over the sound of the rushing wind. She wriggled impatiently, trying to wave to Tor and Mithren, straining at the rope that tied her to the grach's back.

Rowan felt Unos falter. "Annad, be still!" he shouted. Pulling his own bonds, he reached down and rubbed the scaly neck, in the place he had learned the beast liked best. He knew she was very tired. He could almost feel the pain of her exhausted wings and the dryness of her throat. He could almost see the fear lurking behind her fixed eyes.

> *Bound to the beast, you play your part—*
> *The comfort of the aching heart.*

"Good Unos," he crooned in her ear, as he had done so many times before on this long journey. "You will have food soon. More of that pale grass, if Sheba will give it. And cool water, and rest. Do not fear. Just a little farther."

"He is as soft as Grandfather! Does he think the beast understands his words?" Norris's voice floated loud on the wind.

"She understands what he means by them, Nor-ris." Shaaran's voice was far quieter, but Rowan could still hear it.

"Without Rowan's coaxing and his comfort, the beast would have given in and fallen from the sky long ago." That was Allun. "She has not been trained for such a journey. She has not flown at all for many years. She has brought us so far only because Rowan is with us."

So, Sheba, this is my part, Rowan thought hazily. But there is one stick left in the package you gave me. What will it tell me when it burns?

"The people have gathered in the bukshah field," shouted Zeel. "They have weapons. They cannot see us! They think—"

The wind whipped away her last words.

Rowan saw Mithren's kite wheel past him. He saw Mithren's eyes, startled, staring into his. He saw the reed pipe raised to Mithren's lips, and a message sent. He wondered if it would be in time.

20 ∽ TERROR

 "Do not waste arrows, archers," Old Lann was calling. "Aim carefully! Wait for a clear sight!"

For the first time in minutes, Jonn looked up at the hill. Ogden was there no longer. Jonn wondered why.

Jiller and Marlie were in front of him now. All the archers were in front. They were the ones who would try to unseat the riders. The swordsmen, like Jonn, and those with spears were behind. The beast was their target, as were the beasts to come.

The sword was heavy in Jonn's hand. It had been his father's, and had lain idle since the War of the Plains. But now it was to taste Zebak blood again. One last time, perhaps.

The beast was coming. Not like a bolt of lightning, as the first had done, but slowly, as if it was laboring under the weight it carried. Its huge, hideous shape was clear now. Its riders were dark shapes against the sky. There were seven.

"Seven targets," growled Lann. "Seven easy targets."

The kites were still swooping and hovering between the creature and the ground. Why do they not move away? thought Jonn impatiently. They will spoil the archers' aim. Ogden should signal them to retire. Again he glanced up at the hill, but the storyteller had not returned.

From the cloud at the top of the Mountain there was a low grumbling. The Dragon was stirring in its icy palace.

The crowd turned to look, but the archers did not take their eyes from the sky.

"Ready!" called Lann. "When the white kite passes . . ."

The archers raised their drawn bows.

Star was calling from her place in the bukshah circle. Jonn swung around to look at her, puzzled because the sound was not a bellow of fear but a sound of greeting. She was pawing the ground and nodding her head. Again she called. But she did not break the circle.

Jonn heard Lann click her tongue in irritation as

the white kite swooped aside and the red kite immediately took its place between the archers and the beast. Faintly now he could hear Tor and Mithren shouting. And there were other shouts, too, floating thinly in the air. With a shock he realized that the sounds came from the riders. Why would they call out? Unless . . .

"Lann—" he began.

The red kite was caught by a gust of wind and blown upward. At last the target was clear.

"Ready . . ." shouted Lann.

"Stop!"

It was Ogden, waving, running toward them, his high forehead gleaming with sweat. "Put down— your weapons!" he panted as he ran. "I had—a message. The riders—are friends."

Frowning, Lann hesitated. Then— "Wait," she growled to the archers. They froze in position, keeping aim.

"What is this?" she snapped to Ogden. "Friends? How could this be?"

"I do not know." The storyteller gestured at the sky, shaking his head. "The signal was 'Friends! Do not fear.' I ran, to tell you. I knew—you would listen to no one else. Lay down your weapons. Let them land."

"The beast—" Lann began.

But at the same moment Jiller cried out and cast down her bow. Then she was stumbling forward into the shadow of the beast, lifting her arms. "Rowan!" she was crying. "Annad!"

"Allun!" Marlie just whispered the name. She seemed frozen to the spot, her hands still clutching the bow. Her pale face was even whiter than before.

Jonn looked up. And at last he saw what they had seen.

It was beyond his wildest dreams. Roped to the beast's back, bouncing and sliding as it landed on the grass of the bukshah field, were Rowan, Annad, Zeel, Perlain, and Allun.

And between them, already sliding to the ground with the others as their ropes were untied, were two strangers. A fine, strong young man and a delicate-looking girl who looked more like Rowan's sister than fiery little Annad ever would.

Thunderstruck, Jonn watched as Jiller swept her children into her arms and Marlie flew to Allun's side. He heard cool, quiet Perlain shouting like a madman: "We are all alive! Yet Sheba was right! Five did *not* return. Eight returned. Eight!" He felt the people around him surging forward and heard them marveling, cheering. He saw the huge mottled beast lumber to the stream to drink, as the bukshah rumbled warningly. He saw old Lann, as bewildered by joy and astonishment as he, staring at the strangers.

"So," murmured Ogden, beside him. "Rowan has brought them home. I should have trusted in him. In them all. But even I feared." He drew a long breath. "And so, indeed, it was time. But are there only two?"

Jonn swung around, his eyes full of questions. But Ogden had already moved forward, opening his arms to Zeel, clapping Perlain on the back, then courteously drawing Lann toward the strangers.

"These are your people," Jonn heard him say to the old woman. "Pray welcome them, but save all questions for later. Our trial is still to come, I fear."

"Yes!" exclaimed the boy. "The Zebak cannot be far behind us. And there are many."

"How many?" demanded Lann, putting all surprise and questions aside like the old warrior she was.

But as Norris began to answer her, there was a scream from the crowd, and then everyone was pointing.

The horizon was black with flying shapes. Like swarming bees at first, they grew larger and nearer with every blink—a vast army borne on beating, armored wings.

The bukshah bellowed, pawing the ground. The grach by the stream hissed a warning. And the Mountain seemed to tremble with the Dragon's roars. Its fire burned in the cloud, staining the misty white with crimson.

"Positions, archers!" ordered Lann. "Others, get behind!"

"Rowan, look after her!" Jiller cried, thrusting Annad into his arms. "The children are all in the mill. Take her there!"

Then she was gone, running to her place.

The people were lighting new torches, straightening their backs, throwing back their shoulders, and raising their weapons. Allun, Perlain, Zeel, and Norris were joining their ranks with whatever weapons they could find. But Shaaran had backed away to the edge of the field, where a pile of unlit torches lay beside a leaping fire. Her eyes were wide with fear as she stared at the sky, and she clutched the box of silks to her as though somehow it could protect her from harm.

Rowan, too, looked at the sky. It was darkening as the enemy rushed toward them, faster than the wind. There are too many, he thought. Too many.

He pulled Annad over to where Shaaran stood. "You must take Shaaran to the mill, Annad," he urged. "Make haste."

Annad shook her head. "You take her, Rowan," she cried. "I will fight!" Tearing herself away from his grasp, she seized a torch and lit it, brandishing it above her head fiercely.

"Let her do what she wills," said Shaaran. Rowan saw to his amazement that her pale lips were curving into a smile as she watched Annad run back to the field. She glanced at him. "She is so strong and fierce," she explained. "She is like Norris. They all are. It is so strange."

"Not strange here," said Rowan grimly. "Here it is you and I who are the oddities."

Shaaran laughed, turning to him. "Not so odd, if there are two of us," she said.

Rowan felt a terrible ache in his heart. "Shaaran, go to the mill," he begged. "You can find the way—" But even as he spoke, he knew that it was already too late. For now the Zebak army had swept over the hills, and the valley itself was darkening under its shadow.

Shaaran put the box down behind her and lit a torch as Annad had done. "There is no hope, is there, Rowan?" she said sadly.

No hope.

The words rang in Rowan's mind as he fumbled for the oilcloth package inside his shirt and pulled out the last stick.

"Shaaran, hold the torch straight, whatever happens," he said, and he thrust the stick into the flame she held. Pain shot through his arm, and he groaned, but held his hand steady. Shaaran drew a sharp breath as flickering green took the place of red and Sheba's face appeared in the flame. But Shaaran braced one slim arm with the other, so the torch would not tremble as the words came.

> *As fear approaches like the night,*
> *Flee from the field and hide from sight.*
> *The power stirs, the anger wakes,*
> *The rage upon the darkness breaks.*
> *A fearful lesson, learned full well,*
> *A tale that they alone can tell.*

The words ended with a sigh; the flame died. Gasping, Rowan shook his head to clear it, and looked behind him.

The Rin army was still standing fast. Not one person had moved. The roaring from the Mountain was like thunder. The bukshah stood like gray rocks beyond their pool. And it was growing dark. Dark as night. The shadow of the enemy was almost upon them.

Flee from the field and hide from sight. . . .

This time Rowan did not think, did not question. "Take the silks and go into the orchard! Hide in the trees. Make haste!" he called to Shaaran over the noise. Then, shouting at the top of his voice, he ran to the front of the crowd. "Move from here!" he cried, waving his arms. "Run to the orchard!"

The crowd wavered, swaying like grain in a field brushed by the wind.

"Hold your positions!" thundered Lann, scowling in fury.

Rowan spun round to her. "I cannot explain, but I know this is right!" he shouted. "Do not delay! Tell them! *Tell them!*"

As Lann hesitated, Rowan heard a movement behind him. Jiller and Jonn had stepped from their places and were striding toward the orchard. Marlie, Allun, Perlain, Zeel, and Norris were pushing through the crowd to join them, with Timon close behind. And when Bronden, too, began to move, beckoning Val and Ellis to follow, the rest of the crowd wavered no longer but ran for their lives.

In moments the center of the field was empty except for Rowan and Lann, standing face to face.

"We have never run from an enemy till this day, Rowan of the Bukshah," the old woman hissed.

"We are not running from an enemy," Rowan said quietly. "We are clearing the way for—a lesson."

She stared at him.

"Come with me, Lann," he begged. "Come with me, under cover, and you will see."

21 ∽ THE LESSON

"The slaves are scattering! Hiding their snivelling heads!" The commanding officer of the Zebak fleet looked down at the empty field below, smiling with satisfaction. Then he shouted angrily as his grach rolled in the air, nearly unseating him.

"It is the roaring sound and the flashing light from the mountain ahead, sir," shouted the beast's handler. "Bara fears it."

"You fool! What could be in any mountain for a fighting grach to fear?" spat the officer. "Give it a taste of the whip!"

But the handler had no chance to raise the whip, or even to answer. Suddenly there was a roar louder than anything he had ever heard, and the next moment he was clinging to the grach's neck, in fear for his life. And he was shrieking, as the proud man behind him, and the grach itself, were shrieking. In terror.

For the cloud that shrouded the tip of the mountain was swirling aside. And soaring toward them, roaring fire, was something only hinted at in their worst nightmare—a huge, awesome, ice white, ancient thing of gaping jaws, needle-sharp teeth, and terrible, jealous anger.

Compared with this, the ishkin were like writhing worms. The grach were garbage-eating desert lizards. This was a ruler. It was mighty. The earth below was of no interest to it. But the sky was its domain. They had dared to invade its place.

Bara was crying, twisting, plunging, as were all the other grach in that great close-knit fleet. The bonds that held the riders to their seats were breaking like twine. Guards were falling, howling, to the earth below.

And the Dragon roared in savage fury, its breath scorching the earth and the air with tongues of flame.

"Help me!" The handler heard the long scream as his chief plummeted to the shadowed ground he had planned to own. But he could not turn. He could do nothing but cling to Bara's scaly neck as the creature wheeled, hissing, and sped away, back the way it had come. Away from the red eyes and the fire. Away from the burning, jealous anger. Away from the place its masters had thought so easy to conquer, but which had proved to have a guardian that would haunt their dreams forever.

When it was over, the people of Rin crept from their hiding places. All were well. All were safe.

"They will never come again," said Timon. "They have learned a lesson even we did not know. The survivors will spread the word. Our skies are even better protected than our seas."

A fearful lesson, learned full well,
A tale that they alone can tell.

"The Dragon of the Mountain," Lann breathed. "I never thought to see it in my lifetime." She was clinging to Rowan's arm. Her hands were trembling.

The ground where they had stood was scorched black. The bukshah pool still steamed. But the herd was already moving quietly to the stream to drink, the calves were investigating the strange, mottled, but apparently friendly creature that wallowed by the grassy banks, and Star was looking for Rowan.

She saw him, huffed gladly, and broke into a run, blackened earth flying from under her hooves.

"If we had stayed in the field . . ." The whispered words passed from one to the other till the whole crowd was murmuring. "If it had not been for Rowan . . ."

"That you fools were saved was not due to Rowan of the Bukshah, but to me." The rasping voice sawed through the air like a rusty knife.

Unos the grach looked up from her place in the stream. Hissing eagerly, she began to clamber up the bank.

Sheba stalked from the shade of the orchard trees. Her oily hair swung around her face like rats' tails. Her ragged clothes smelled of ash and dust and bitter herbs.

"Come here, skinny rabbit!" she commanded.

Rowan left Star with Lann and walked slowly toward the old woman. He felt Unos lumber up behind him, snuffling the air with pleasure. People drew back on all sides, shuddering at the sight of her.

"And so you have come back, Rowan of the Bukshah," Sheba screeched. "You and your foolish company of oddities, with two more oddities towed along behind."

She cast a mocking glance at Norris and Shaaran. Norris scowled, and Shaaran shrank back. Sheba cackled with laughter.

"You were with us, Sheba," said Allun quietly.

"And a fine dance you led me," she mumbled. "Days and nights of watching. Days and nights without food or drink or sleep . . ."

"We owe you a great debt," said Rowan.

"Yes!" Sheba jeered. "And I have come to claim it!" She held up a crumpled note. "Written in your own hand!" she crowed. "Your promised gift!"

Rowan looked down to the stream where the black bukshah calf played and bounded with its friends, and it was as if bony fingers clutched at his heart. But he had promised.

He turned back to Sheba. "I had not forgotten," he said.

She grinned, showing all her long brown teeth. "But as it happens, I have changed my mind about the companion I prefer," she said. "I find the idea of the calf bores me. There have been other black calves in the herd. I have a fancy for—this."

She pointed to the grach.

Rowan glanced at Shaaran and Norris. Norris shrugged. Shaaran watched as Unos lowered her lumpy head and rubbed the old woman's hand, and then she nodded. "Her name is Unos," she said.

"Very good. She will be a proper companion for me." Sheba stroked the grach's mottled neck with strange gentleness. "She is a true oddity."

"Not where I have come from," Norris said loudly.

"Here Unos is rare," Ogden said. "And what is rare is always precious." He put his hand on Zeel's shoulder as he spoke, but his dark gaze moved over the faces of Perlain, Allun, Shaaran, and Rowan, and he smiled.

Sheba sniffed and hobbled away, clicking her tongue to Unos as she went. The grach plodded after her, hissing contentedly.

"It is good. Unos will be happy with her." Shaaran sighed, looking after them. But her eyes had filled with tears. Rowan knew that she was thinking of her grandfather, feeling lost. He felt Star's nose nudging his shoulder and turned to pat her. Star, at least, was relieved to see the grach go out of her sight. But Shaaran . . .

"So we have found a home for one of our new citizens," said Allun from his place in the crowd. "What of the others?"

He and Marlie came forward with his mother, Sara, beaming between them.

"My mother is not much of an oddity," Allun said to Norris and Shaaran. "The only odd thing she ever did in her life was marry a Traveler, and she paid dearly for that by having me for a son. But soon she will be like a bird who has lost her only chick, for Marlie has foolishly agreed to marry me."

He looked around, grinning at the murmur of surprise and congratulation that rose from the crowd and ignoring Marlie's kick on his ankle. Then he turned again to Shaaran and Norris.

"The wedding will be very soon. Before Marlie can come to her senses and change her mind," he went on. "So mother begs you both to come and fill her nest. After all, *someone* must weed her garden. And she is an excellent cook."

Sara smiled comfortably at Norris and Shaaran, who were both looking stunned. "Take no notice of my son's foolishness!" she said. "But I would very much like to have you, if you would like to come."

Shaaran glanced at Norris and saw his face break into a broad grin. She turned to Sara. "Thank you," she said shyly. "We would like it, very much."

Allun rubbed his hands. "So it is settled," he said gleefully. "And now, food! Dried fish and seaweed biscuit are all very well, but bread, cheese, and cakes are better."

"That is a matter of taste," Perlain said, moving quietly up beside him with Zeel. "But I will make do with cheese, once I have soaked for a while, for I am extremely hungry. Indeed, I could eat a whole serpent at a gulp, if it was offered."

The people standing nearby snorted with surprised laughter as they began to move toward the village. It was a small joke, but they had not realized that a Maris could joke at all.

Carrying the box of silks, Rowan walked behind with Jonn, Jiller, Annad, and Shaaran. Annad was dancing impatiently, chattering, pulling on Shaaran's hand to make her move faster. Jiller was laughing, glowing with happiness.

But Jonn was looking in puzzlement from Shaaran's face to Rowan's.

"You have much to tell us, I think, Rowan of Rin," he murmured.

Rowan looked down at the box of silks in his arms and was filled with quiet contentment.

"Yes," he said. "We have much to tell you."